Enid Blyton's

CHIMNEY CORNER
STORIES

Shreelatha Raman

Shreelatha

Raman

Shreelatha

Raman

Enid Blyton's
CHIMNEY CORNER
STORIES

PRINTED IN GREAT BRITAIN
DEAN & SON Ltd.
41/43 Ledgate Hill LONDON S·E·4

Made and printed in Great Britain by Purnell and
Sons, Ltd., Paulton (Somerset) and London

603 03256 7

CONTENTS

The Clockwork Mouse

THERE was once a little boy called Gerry, who was very kind to his toys. He didn't break them. He didn't leave them out in the rain. He really did look after them, and love them.

So they loved him, too. But most of all the clockwork mouse loved Gerry. You see, the clockwork mouse had once lost his key, so he couldn't be wound up, and that made him very unhappy. He did so love to run about, and if he wasn't wound up he couldn't.

Nobody ever knew how he lost his key. It just disappeared. The golliwog thought that it might have dropped out on the floor, and been swept up in the carpet-sweeper.

"Then it would go into the dustbin with the rubbish," said the Teddy. "And that would be the end of it."

Then Gerry noticed that the mouse hadn't a key. "Where's your key?" he said. "I'll wind you up and give you a run."

The mouse looked sadly up at him. He couldn't have a run round the nursery, looking for crumbs, because his key was lost.

"Why, your key is gone!" said Gerry, and he hunted about for it. But he couldn't find it. "Never mind," said Gerry. "I'll do something about it, mouse. I can see by your face that you feel sad about it. I know how I should feel if I could only run when I was wound up—and suddenly lost my key!"

Well, Gerry went to such a lot of trouble to get the mouse a new key. He went to the toy-shop and asked for one, but they said they couldn't take keys out of any of the animals there. So that wasn't any good.

Then he had a good idea, and went to the clock-shop—and a little key there fitted the mouse exactly! Wasn't that lucky?

The mouse was so very pleased to be able to run about again that when the golly wound him up that night he tore round as fast as an express train! The dolls' house dolls gave a little party to show how glad they were, and everyone was happy.

The mouse couldn't say enough about Gerry because he was so happy at having a new key. "He's a wonderful boy," he kept saying to everyone. "He's marvellous! Fancy bothering about a little mouse like me! If only I could do something for him one day! But I'm too little to be of any real use to Gerry."

Now one day Gerry came into the nursery as excited as could be.

"Hallo, toys!" he said. "What do you think? I'm going on the bus to my cousin Billy's all by myself! My, I'm getting grown-up, I can tell you! Look, I've got my purse with the bus-fare in."

The toys all stared up at the little brown leather purse. It had a silver sixpence in.

"I've got to change my shoes, and then I'm ready."

He put his purse down beside his feet on the floor, and then began to put on his walking shoes. He was soon ready.

"Hurry!" called his mother. "You don't want to miss the bus, Gerry."

Gerry stood up, and then ran out of the room. The toys heard him running down the passage to the garden door, shouting good-bye to his mother.

And then the golly saw that he had left the little brown purse on the floor! He had forgotten it—and inside was the money for the bus. Oh dear—now what was to be done?

"He'll not be able to pay for his ticket," said the golliwog. "He'll not be able to go."

"Poor Gerry," said the teddy bear, sadly.

"What a disappointment," said the clown.

"I'm going after him!" cried the clockwork mouse, in his high squeaky voice. "Wind me up, Golly. Tie the purse on to my back, Teddy. Hurry!"

Whilst the golly was winding him up, the teddy tied the little purse firmly on to the small mouse's back. Then off he rushed out of the door, down the passage, out of the garden door, down the path, and into the street!

You should have seen him go! He had never run so fast in his life. He really whirred along. Far in front of him was Gerry.

The mouse panted along, hoping he would catch the boy. Suddenly Gerry stopped and clapped his hand to his pocket.

He had suddenly remembered his purse. He had left it behind. He stared in dismay, for he could see the bus coming round the corner!

And at that very moment something brushed against his shoe! It was the little mouse! Gerry looked down and stared in the greatest surprise. He saw the purse at once and pulled it off the mouse's back.

"I can't believe it!" he kept saying to himself. "I can't

believe it. You can't really have come after me with my
purse—and yet you have!"

He hadn't time to do anything more than take the purse,
for the bus was stopping. He rushed off—and the clockwork
mouse watched him get on the bus. The little creature was
very happy.

"I've been of some real use to Gerry at last," he said,
and ran happily back home.

And on the way home he had an adventure—yes, a real
adventure! A cat saw him running by and thought he was
a real mouse. She sprang after him and he tore away as fast
as ever he could.

In at the gate he went, down the path and through the
garden door. And there his clockwork ran down—but the
golly was waiting for him and wound him up again. So he
was able to run safely into the nursery and stop there, panting
and excited, to tell his adventures.

Everyone praised him and made a fuss of him. "You ought
to have a medal, or something," said the golly.

Well, he did have something! Gerry brought home a little
red ribbon and tied it round his neck.

"That's to show you are the best clockwork mouse in the
world!" he said. And dear me, wasn't the mouse proud!
He's still got that ribbon, and he'll tell you why, if you ask
him.

Winkle-Pip Walks Out

ONCE upon a time Winkle-Pip the gnome did a good turn to the Tappetty Witch, and she was very grateful. "I will give you something," she said. "Would you like a wishing-suit?"

"Ooh, yes!" cried Winkle-Pip, delighted. "That would be lovely."

So the Tappetty Witch gave Winkle-Pip a wishing-suit. It was made of yellow silk, spotted with red, and had big pockets in it.

"Now," said the witch to Winkle-Pip, "whenever you wear this suit, your wishes will come true—but there is one thing you must do, Winkle."

"What's that?" asked Winkle-Pip.

"Once each year you must go out into the world of boys and girls and grant wishes to six of them," said the witch. "Now don't forget that, Winkle, or the magic will go out of your wishing-suit."

Winkle-Pip promised not to forget, and off he went home, with the wishing-suit wrapped up in brown paper, tucked safely under his arm.

Now the next day Winkle-Pip's old Aunt Maria was coming to see him. She always liked a very good tea, and often grumbled because Winkle-Pip, who was not a very good cook, sometimes gave her burnt cakes, or jam sandwich that hadn't risen well, and was all wet and heavy.

So the gnome decided to use his wishing-suit the next day, and give his aunt a wonderful surprise. He put it on in the morning and looked at himself in the glass—and he looked very nice indeed. He thought he would try the wish-magic, so he put his hands in his pockets and spoke aloud.

"I wish for a fine feathered cap to go with my suit!" he said.

Hey presto! A yellow hat with a red feather came from nowhere, and landed with a thud on his big head.

"Ho!" said Winkle-Pip, pleased. "That's a real beauty."

He looked round his kitchen. It was not very clean, and none of the breakfast dishes had been washed up. The curtains looked dirty too, and Winkle-Pip remembered that his Aunt Maria had said he really should wash them.

"Now for a bit of fun!" said Winkle, and he put his hands in his pockets again.

"Kitchen, tidy yourself, for that is my wish!" he said, loudly.

At once things began to stir and hum. The tap ran water, and the dishes jumped about in the bowl and washed themselves. The cloth jumped out of the pail under the sink, and rubbed itself hard on the soap. Then it began to wash the kitchen floor far more quickly than Winkle-Pip had ever been able to do.

The brush leapt out of its corner and swept the rugs, which were really very dirty indeed. The pan held itself ready for the sweepings, and when it was full it ran outside to the dustbin, and emptied itself there.

You should have seen the kitchen when everything had quieted down again ! How it shone and glittered ! Even the saucepans had joined in and had let themselves be scrubbed well in the sink. It was marvellous.

" Now for the curtains ! " said Winkle-Pip, and he put his hands in his pockets again. " I wish you to make yourselves clean ! " he called.

The curtains didn't need to be told twice. They sprang off their hooks and rushed to the sink. The tap ran and filled the basin with hot water. The soap made a lather, and then those curtains jumped themselves up and down in the water until every speck of dirt had run from them and they were as white as snow ! Then they flew to the mangle, which squeezed the water from them. Then out to the line in the yard they went, and the pegs pegged them there in the wind. The wind blew its hardest, and in a few minutes they flew back into the kitchen once more. The iron had already put itself on the stove to heat, and as soon as the curtains appeared and laid themselves flat on the table, the iron jumped over to them and ironed them out beautifully.

Then back to their hooks they flew, and hung themselves up at the windows. How lovely they looked !

" Wonderful ! " cried Winkle-Pip in delight. " My, I wonder what my old Aunt Maria will say ! "

Then he began to think about food.

"I think I'll have a big chocolate cake, a jelly with sliced pears in it, a dozen little ginger cakes, some ham sandwiches, some fresh lettuce and radishes, and some raspberries and cream," decided Winkle. "That would make a simply glorious tea!"

So he wished for all those—and you should just have seen his kitchen coming to life again. It didn't take the magic very long to make all the cakes and sandwiches he wanted, and to wash the lettuce and radishes that suddenly flew in from the garden.

"Splendid!" cried the gnome, clapping his hands with joy. "Won't my Aunt Maria stare to see all this?"

In the afternoon his old aunt came—and as soon as she opened the kitchen door, how she stared! She looked at the snowy sink, she looked at the spotless floor. She stared at the clean curtains, and she stared at the shining saucepans. Then she gazed at the lovely tea spread out on the table.

"Well!" she cried in astonishment. "What a marvellous change, Winkle-Pip. How hard you must have worked! I am really very, very pleased with you."

She gave the gnome a loud kiss, and he blushed very red.

"It's my wishing-suit, Aunt," he said, for he was a truthful little gnome. He told her all about it and she was full of surprise.

"Well, you be sure to take great care of it," she said, eating a big piece of chocolate cake. "And whatever you do, Winkle-Pip, don't forget to go out into the world of boys and girls and find six of them to grant wishes to—or you'll lose the wishing-magic as sure as eggs are eggs."

Winkle-Pip *did* enjoy his wishing-suit! He granted wishes to all his friends—and you may be sure that everyone wanted to be his friend when they knew about his new magic suit! Then a time came when he knew that he must go out into our world, for the magic in his suit began to weaken.

So one day Winkle-Pip put on his suit of yellow silk and his fine feathered cap, and walked to the end of Fairyland.

"How pleased all the boys and girls will be to see me!" he said. "And how glad they will be to have their wishes granted. I am sure they don't see fairy folk very often, and they will go mad with joy to find me walking up to them."

"Don't be too sure," said his friend, the green pixie, who had walked to the gates of Fairyland with him. "I have heard that boys and girls nowadays don't believe in fairies, and are much too busy with their wireless-sets and their Meccanos to want to listen to tales about us. They might not believe in you!"

"Rubbish!" said Winkle. He shook hands with the green pixie and walked out into our world. He looked all around him and wondered which way to go.

"I'll go eastwards," he thought. "It looks as if there might be a town over there."

So off he went, and after a few miles he came to a little market town. He went along, peeping into the windows of the houses as he passed by, and at last he saw a nursery. A little boy and girl were playing with a beautiful dolls' house, and they were talking about it.

"You know, this dolls' house is very old-fashioned," said the little boy. "It's got oil-lamps, instead of electric light. It's a silly dolls' house, I think."

"Well, I'm sure Grandpa won't have electric light put into it for us," said the little girl. "I do so wish he would. That would be fine!"

"Ha!" thought Winkle-Pip. "Here's a chance for me to give them a wish."

So he jumped into the window, and walked quietly up behind the children. "Would you like electric light in that dolls' house?" he asked. "You have only to wish for it, whilst I am here, and you shall have it."

The children looked round in surprise.

"Of course I'd like it," said the girl. "I wish I *could* have electric light all over the house!"

In a second the magic had worked, and the dolls' house was lit up with tiny electric lights from top to bottom! How the children gasped to see such a wonderful sight. They found that there were tiny switches beside each door, and when they snapped these on and off the lights went on or out. They began to play with them in great excitement.

Meanwhile the gnome stood behind them, waiting for a word of thanks. The children seemed quite to have forgotten him. He was terribly hurt, and at last he crept out of the window, without even saying good-bye.

"Fancy not thanking me for granting their wish!" he thought, mournfully. "Well, that was a nasty surprise for me! I thought the children would be delighted to talk to me too."

Winkle-Pip went on again, and after a while he came across two boys hunting in the grass for something they had lost.

"Where *can* that shilling have gone?" he heard one of them say. "Oh, I do wish we could find it, for we shall get into such trouble for losing it, when we get home."

Up went Winkle-Pip to them. "I can grant you your wish," he said. "I am a gnome, and have my wishing-suit on."

The two boys looked at him.

"Don't be silly," said one. "You know quite well that there are no such things as gnomes—and as for wishing-suits, well, you *must* think us stupid to believe in things like that! You couldn't possibly grant us a wish!"

Winkle-Pip went very red. He stuck his hands in his pockets and looked at the two boys.

"Do you really want to find that shilling?" he asked.

"Yes, rather!" said the boys. "We wish we could, for we shall get whipped for coming home without it."

No sooner had they wished than the silver shilling rose up from where it had been hidden in the grass, and flew into Winkle-Pip's hand.

"Here it is," he said to the boys, and gave it to them. But were they pleased? No, not a bit of it!

"You had it all the time!" they cried, for they had not seen it fly into the gnome's hand. "You have played a trick on us! We will beat you."

They set upon the poor gnome and he had to run for his life. He sat down on the first gate he came to and rubbed his bruises.

"Well!" he thought miserably. "That's two wishes granted and not a word of thanks for either of them. What is the world coming to, I wonder? Is there any politeness or gratitude left?"

After a while he went on again, and soon he heard the sound of sobbing. He peeped round the corner and saw a little girl sitting on the steps of a small house, crying bitterly.

"What's the matter?" asked Winkle-Pip, his kind heart touched by her loud sobs. At first the little girl didn't answer, but just frowned at him. Then suddenly from the house there came a voice.

"Now stop that silly crying, Mary! You deserved to be smacked. It was very naughty of you to break your poor dolly like that, just out of temper."

"I shall break her again if I like!" shouted the naughty little girl, jumping to her feet and stamping hard. The gnome was terribly shocked.

"You shouldn't talk like that," he said. "Why, do you know, I came to give you a wish, and——"

"Silly creature, silly creature!" screamed the bad-tempered child, making an ugly face at him. "I wish you'd go away, that's what I wish! I wish you'd run to the other end of the town; then I wouldn't see you any more!"

Well, of course, her wish had to come true and poor Winkle-Pip found himself scurrying off to the other end of the town in a mighty hurry. He was soon very much out of breath, but not until he was right at the other end of the little town did his feet stop running.

"My goodness!" said Winkle-Pip, sinking down on the grass by the road-side. "What a horrid day I'm having! What nasty children there are nowadays! Three more wishes to give away—and, dear me, I do wish I'd finished, for I'm not enjoying it at all."

As Winkle-Pip sat there, two children came by, a boy and a girl.

"Hallo, funny-face," said the boy, rudely. "Wherever do you come from?"

"I come from Fairyland," said the gnome. "I am a gnome, as I should think you could guess."

"Pooh!" said the boy, "what rubbish to talk like that! There are no gnomes or fairies."

"Of course not," said the little girl.

"Well, there *are*," said Winkle-Pip, "and, what's more, I'm rather a special gnome. I've come into your world to-day to give wishes to six children. I've wasted three wishes, and I'm beginning to think there are no children worth bothering about nowadays."

"What, do you mean you can grant wishes to us?" asked the boy. "I don't believe it! Well, I'll try, anyway, and we'll see if what you say is true! I wish for a banana, a pear, and a pineapple to come and sit on your head!"

Whee-ee-ee-ee-eesh! Through the air came flying a large banana, very ripe, a big pear, and a spiky pineapple. Plonk! They all fell on poor Winkle-Pip's head and he groaned in dismay. The children stared in amazement and began to laugh. Then they looked rather scared.

"Ooh!" said the boy. "He must be a gnome, after all, because our wish came true!"

Winkle-Pip was so angry that he couldn't think what to say. The children gave him one more look and then took to their heels and fled, afraid of what the gnome might do to them in revenge.

Poor Winkle-Pip! He was so distressed and so hurt to think that children could play him such a mean trick when he had offered them a wish, that he hardly knew what to do. He tried his best to get the fruit off his head, but it was so firmly stuck there that it would not move.

"Oh dear! oh dear!" wept the gnome. "I shall have to let it all stay there, because I can't have any wishes for myself till I have given away the six wishes to boys and girls."

Presently there came by a little girl carrying a heavy load of wood. She stopped when she saw the gnome, and looked at him in surprise.

"Why are you carrying all those things on your head?" she asked. "Aren't they dreadfully heavy?"

"Yes," said the gnome with a sigh. "But I can't very well help it." Then he told the little girl all his story, and she was very sorry for him.

"I do wish I could get it off for you," she said. "If I had a wish, I would wish that, and the fruit would fly away."

No sooner had she spoken these words than her wish came true! Off flew the banana, off went the pear, and off jumped the pineapple. They all disappeared with a click, and the gnome shook his head about in joy.

"Hurrah!" he said. "They've gone. Oh, you nice little girl, I'm so glad you wished that wish. You're the only unselfish child I have met in my journeys to-day."

"And you're the first person who has ever called me unselfish," said the little girl, with a sigh. "I live with my stepmother, and she is always telling me I am lazy and selfish. I do try so hard not to be."

"Poor child," said Winkle-Pip, thinking it was a dreadful shame to make a little girl carry such a heavy load of wood. "Have you no kind father?"

"No," said the little girl. "I have an aunt though, but since we moved she doesn't know where my stepmother and I live. My stepmother didn't like her because she was kind to me, and wanted me to live with her. She said I was nothing but a little servant to my stepmother, and so I am. I wouldn't mind that a bit, if only she would love me and be kind to me."

Winkle-Pip was nearly in tears when he heard this sad story. "I do wish I could help you," he said. "What a pity your kind aunt isn't here to take you to her home and love you."

"I do wish she was," said the little girl, lifting the bundle of wood on to her shoulder again—and then she gave a loud cry of delight and dropped it. Winkle-Pip cried out too, for, what do you think?—hurrying towards them was the kindest, plumpest woman you could possibly imagine!

"Auntie! Auntie!" cried the little girl. "I was just wishing you were here!"

"Of course," said Winkle-Pip to himself with a smile, "that's the sixth wish! I'd quite forgotten there was still another one to give. Well, I'm very, very glad that this little girl has got the last wish. She used up one wish to set me free from that banana, pear, and pineapple, and she deserves to have one for herself, bless her kind heart!"

"Where have you come from, Auntie?" asked the little girl, hugging the smiling woman round the neck. "Oh, I *have* missed you so!"

"I've come to fetch you home with me," said her aunt, kissing her. "I've had such a time trying to find out where your stepmother took you to. I don't quite know how I got here, but still, here I am, and you're coming straight home with me, and I'm going to look after you and love you."

" But what about my stepmother ? " asked the child.

" Oh, I'll go and see her for you," said the gnome, with a grin. " I'll tell her what I think of her. You go home with your aunt and have a lovely time. I'll take your wood back for you."

So the little girl went off happily, with her aunt holding her

tightly by the hand. Winkle-Pip shouldered the bundle of wood and ran off to the little cottage that the child had pointed out to him.

An ugly, bad-tempered-looking woman opened the door, and frowned when she saw Winkle-Pip.

" I've brought you the wood that your little stepdaughter was bringing," said the gnome. " She has gone to live with her auntie."

" Oh, she has, has she ? " said the woman, picking up a

broom. " Well, I'm sure *you've* had something to do with that, you interfering little creature ! I'll give you such a drubbing ! "

She ran at the little gnome, but he stuck his hands into his pockets, and wished quickly.

" I've given away six wishes ! " he said. " Now my wishing-suit is full of magic for me again—so I wish myself back in Fairyland once more ! "

Whee-ee-ee-eesh ! He was swept up into the air, and vanished before the angry woman's eyes. She turned pale with fright, and ran inside her cottage and banged the door. She was so terrified that she never once tried to find out where her stepdaughter had gone.

As for Winkle-Pip, he was delighted to get home again.

Over a cup of cocoa he told the green pixie all his adventures, and they both agreed that he had had a most exciting day.

It will soon be time for Winkle-Pip to walk out into our world again—so be careful if you meet him, and do try to use your wish in the best way you can.

Trit-Trot the Pony

THERE was once a brown pony called Trit-Trot. It belonged to old Mrs. Kennedy, and she used it for pulling her little pony-cart along when she went shopping. But, as she didn't go shopping very often, Trit-Trot spent a good deal of time alone in the field.

Every day, as he went to and from school, a boy called Billy stopped to speak to the pony. " Hallo, Trit-Trot ! " he would say. " How are you to-day ? Found any nice grass to eat ? I'll bring you my apple-core to munch when I've eaten the apple at school this morning."

He always remembered to do as he said, and Trit-Trot liked Billy very much. He thought he was the nicest boy he had ever met. Some of the boys that came by were not so nice.

" There's Leonard—he once threw a stone at me," thought the brown pony, as he ate the grass. " And there's that nasty big boy called Harry—he has tried to catch me and ride me heaps of times. I wouldn't at all mind giving him a ride— but he always has a big stick to hit me with, and I won't have that ! Ah—Billy's the nicest. Always a kind word for a lonely little pony, and sometimes a juicy carrot, and apple—or even a lump of sugar saved from his breakfast cocoa ! He really is a friend to have. I wish I could do something to pay him back for his kindness."

Now one day, when Billy was standing on the field-gate talking to Trit-Trot, the big boy called Harry came along.

"Hallo, Billy!" he said. "Got any money to-day? There's some fine new marbles in the toy-shop."

"I've got three pennies and a ha'penny," said Billy. "But I'm saving them up for my mother's birthday."

"Well, lend them to me till Saturday, and I'll get the marbles," said Harry.

"No," said Billy. "I lent you a penny last month, and you never gave it back to me."

"What! You won't lend me the money to get the marbles!" cried Harry, angrily. "We'll see about that. I can easily get them away from a little shrimp like you!"

And before Billy could shout or say a word, Harry had him down off the gate, and had taken the little purse from his pocket. He emptied the money out, put it loose into his own pocket, and threw the purse back to Billy. It wasn't a bit of good Billy trying to get his money back. Harry was far too big and fierce to fight.

Harry went off whistling. Billy stared after him, angry and miserable. Trit-Trot the pony watched from surprised brown eyes. Billy turned to him and stroked his long nose.

"It's too bad," he said. "I shan't get that money back. I know I shan't. It took me three-and-a-half weeks to save it."

Trit-Trot was sorry. He didn't like Harry any more than Billy did. He suddenly left the gate and ran down the field. At the end of it there was a gap that he could just squeeze through. Trit-Trot squashed his fat little brown body through it, and then stood waiting for Harry to come by. Ah—there he was, whistling merrily. Harry stopped when he saw Trit-Trot. "Hallo!" he said. "You've got out of the field. Give me a ride, will you? Come on!" Usually Trit-Trot ran away when Harry came near— but now he stood still, and let Harry get on to his back. "Gee-up!" said Harry, and hit the pony with the stick he always carried.

The pony trotted off to the opposite side of the road, where there was a muddy patch. He suddenly stopped still, gave himself a jerk and off went Harry, landing in the mud with a bump and a splash. Trit-Trot neighed. Then he bent down his big head, and took hold of Harry's belt with his strong teeth. Harry screamed. He half-thought the pony was going to eat him! But Trit-Trot had another idea in his mind! He carried the wriggling boy down the lane to the field-gate, where Billy was still standing.

"Hrrrumph!" said Trit-Trot, still holding Harry tightly by his belt.

"Trit-Trot! You've caught Harry—and brought him to me!" cried Billy, with a laugh, for really Harry looked very funny. "I suppose you thought I could get back my money if you held him like that for me. Well—I can!"

And Billy quickly took back the money Harry had taken from him, and put it safely in his purse. Then Trit-Trot dropped Harry on to the ground and looked at Billy, asking him with big brown eyes to open the gate and let him into his field once more.

Harry jumped to his feet and fled down the lane at top speed. He was afraid Trit-Trot would go after him and grab him again. He disappeared round the bend and Billy gave a sigh of relief!

"Thank you, Trit-Trot," he said. "You really are a good friend! I'm sure Mother won't believe me when she hears what you did!"

"Hrrrr-umph!" said Trit-Trot, rubbing his nose against Billy's arm. Billy knew what that meant quite well—he was saying: "I've paid you back for your kindness!" And he certainly had, hadn't he?

B

The Magic Walking-stick

TELL-TALE TIPPY was a pixie that nobody liked, and his name will tell you why. He told a hundred tales a day about other people—horrid, sneaky tales—and made all his friends very unhappy.

"Can't we do something to stop Tippy from telling tales?" asked Gobo the elf. "He would be quite nice if only he hadn't that nasty habit."

But it wasn't a bit of use—scolding and coaxing made no difference to Tippy. He just went on telling tales.

"Gobo went shopping with a hole in his stocking this morning!" he told everybody.

"Pippit hasn't got enough money to pay his chocolate bill this week!" he whispered.

"Silverwing hasn't been asked to Tiptoe's party," he said. Wasn't he mean? It is so horrid to tell tales and, really, Tippy had a new tale to tell almost every minute, so sharp were his little green eyes, and so long was the nose that he poked into everyone's business.

Aha! But he did it once too often, as you will see!

When the Enchanter Too-Tall came to Tippy's village to see his old Aunt Mickle-Muckle, Tippy was delighted—because, you see, Mrs. Mickle-Muckle lived next door to Tippy, and he could spy on all that the Enchanter did.

Now Too-Tall the Enchanter had a habit of getting up very early in the morning, and walking in the garden in his dressing-gown to get the fresh, cool air. Tippy heard him and crept to the window.

There, down below in Mrs. Mickle-Muckle's little garden,

was Too-Tall the Enchanter, his mass of curly hair blowing in the morning breeze.

And, as Tippy watched, what do you think happened? Why, the enchanter's hair all blew away in the wind, every single bit of it! And Tippy saw that he was quite bald.

"Ooh! He wears a wig! He wears a wig!" said the peeping pixie. "I never knew that before! Why, he is as bald as a pea! Oh look! His curly wig has blown into the big rose-bush!"

Too-Tall the Enchanter was horrified when his wig blew off. He looked round hurriedly to see if anyone was about who might see his bald head, but he couldn't spy Tippy, who was safely behind his curtain. Quickly he ran to the rose-bush and pulled out his wig, which had settled down right in the middle of it. He scratched his hands on the prickles and said, very loudly, "Oh, bother! *Bother!* BOTHER!"

Then he put his wig on his head again, rather crooked, and went indoors.

Tippy rubbed his hands in glee. What a lovely tale he would have to tell everyone that morning! He dressed very quickly, had his breakfast, put on his pointed cap, and went out. The first person he met was Gobo the elf, and he ran up to him.

"Gobo, listen! Too-Tall the Enchanter is as bald as a pea! His hair is a wig! It blew off this morning and he said ' Bother! *Bother!* BOTHER!'"

" Ooh ! " said Gobo, surprised. " But really, Tippy, you shouldn't tell tales, you know. You've been told ever so often. Too-Tall would be awfully cross if he knew you had told about his bald head."

" Pooh ! He'll never know," said Tippy, and he ran off to tell Skippy-Wee the brownie, who was just coming out of his cottage.

" Skippy-Wee ! Listen ! Too-Tall the Enchanter is as bald as a pea ! His hair is a wig ! It blew off this morning and he said ' Bother ! *Bother !* Bother ! ' "

" Ooh ! " said Skippy-Wee, with wide-open eyes. " Fancy that ! I always thought he had such curly hair—but, Tippy, Too-Tall would be very angry if he knew you were telling tales about what you saw."

" Pooh ! He'll never know," said Tippy, and ran off to tell his news to someone else.

Well, he told his tale to forty-two different people that morning, and one of them happened to go to tea with Mrs. Mickle-Muckle's old gardener that afternoon. As soon as the gardener heard the tale he went straight to Mrs. Mickle-Muckle and asked her if it were true that her nephew, the great enchanter, hadn't a single hair on his head.

" Ooh my, who told you that ? " said Mrs. Mickle-Muckle. " Well, as far as I know, Too-Tall's hair is his own. I never knew he wore a wig."

Now it so happened that the enchanter's sharp ears heard every word of this, and he went red right down to his collar. Oh, dear! He hadn't wanted anyone to know that he wore a wig—and now it seemed that all the village knew it! He had lost his hair because of a powerful spell that went wrong, and he had had a curly wig made just exactly like the hair he had lost—and he hadn't told a single person about it!

" Who's been telling tales ? " he wondered, with a frown. " Well, I'll find out."

He took a large silver ball and set it on the table in front of him. Then he stroked it with a peacock's feather and sang in a low voice a little magic spell. At the end of it he struck the ball with the feather and said loudly :

" Now let the face of the tell-tale appear ! "

And, gracious goodness, what a very strange and peculiar thing ! In the silver ball came a misty face, and as the enchanter stared at it, it came clearer and clearer, and there at last was Tell-Tale Tippy's face !

" What is your name ? " asked the enchanter.

" Tippy," said the face in the silver ball.

" Where do you live ? " asked the enchanter, sternly.

" Next door," answered the face. Then the enchanter struck the ball with the peacock's feather and the face gradually grew misty and then vanished. Too-Tall put the ball on to a shelf and sat down to think.

Oho ! So it was that nasty little Tippy next door who had seen his wig blow off that morning and had told everyone about it ! The horrid little tell-tale ! His aunt, Mrs. Mickle-Muckle, had often told him what a tell-tale Tippy was—and, really, it was about time that pixie was punished.

The next day Too-Tall the Enchanter went to a shop that sold walking-sticks. He bought one with a crook handle and took it home. It was a really beautiful stick, bright red with a yellow crook, and round the neck of the stick was a silver collar. If you twisted the crook the handle came right off. It was really a very fine stick indeed.

Too-Tall took it home to his aunt's. He unscrewed the handle, and put a funny little blue spell into the neck of the stick. Then he put on the handle once more, screwed it up, hung the stick over his arm, and went next door to see Tippy.

Tippy opened the door himself, and wasn't he surprised to see Too-Tall! He began to shake at the knees, because he knew that he had been telling tales about the enchanter's wig. But Too-Tall didn't frown, and he didn't scold—no, he simply bowed politely, and held out the bright-red stick to Tippy.

" I hear you are a tale-teller," he said. " Pray accept this stick from me—it is one that all tale-tellers should use ! "

Tippy was almost scared out of his life ! He knew that the stick must be a magic one, and he was afraid to take it—but he was also afraid to refuse it ! So he just stood there, trembling, his mouth opening and shutting like a goldfish, not knowing what to do.

The enchanter stood the stick in Tippy's umbrella-stand, and walked back to his aunt's cottage. Tippy stood in the hall, very much afraid of the stick. But it seemed quite harmless. It didn't do anything, or say anything, so suddenly Tippy made a face at it.

" Pooh ! " he said. " You needn't think I'm afraid of you ! I shan't take you out with me, and I shan't take any notice of you at all—so you won't be able to do anything to me, you silly old stick ! "

The stick stood still and said nothing. And just then there came another knock at the door. Tippy opened it, and outside stood Gobo the elf.

" Oh, Tippy," he said, " I've brought back the book you lent me. Thank you very much."

" Oh, thanks," said Tippy. " I say—do you see that blot of ink on the cover ? Well, Skippy-Wee did that when I lent him the book. Wasn't it careless of him ? "

"Oh, don't tell tales," began Gobo—and then he stopped in surprise! The red-and-yellow stick had jumped out of its stand and was whipping Tippy! And all the time it cried out loudly: "Tell-Tale Tippy! Tell-Tale Tippy!"

Tippy howled in pain and ran into the kitchen, but the stick followed him there, and not until he said he was sorry he had told tales did it stop hitting him and go quietly to its stand.

"Ooh my, Tippy, you'd better be careful!" said Gobo the elf. "That stick will make you black and blue if you tell any more tales. I say! Won't everyone laugh when they hear about your stick?"

"Oh, don't tell anyone; please, don't tell anyone!" begged Tippy. "They would laugh at me so."

" Well, you are always telling tales about other people,"
said Gobo. " Why shouldn't I tell tales about *you*, Tippy ? "
And out he went, laughing to himself.

Tippy frowned hard at the magic stick. Then he suddenly
ran at it, grabbed it from the stand, and flung it out of the back
door into the garden. He slammed the door, and cried out :
" Stay there, you miserable thing ! "

He put the kettle on to make some cocoa, for he really felt
quite ill—and then he heard a tap-tap-tapping upstairs. The
tap-tap-tap came all the way down the stairs, and, goodness me,
when Tippy looked out into the hall, there was the magic stick
back in the umbrella-stand again ! It had crept in at one of the
bedroom windows and gone back to the stand by itself.

After he had had a drink of hot cocoa, Tippy thought he
had better go and do some shopping. So he put on his pointed
cap and out he went—but as he passed through the hall the
stick jumped from the hall-stand and quietly hooked itself on
Tippy's arm ! He didn't notice it, and went walking on with
the stick beside him.

Soon he met Mrs. Cuddle, the balloon woman, and he
stopped to speak to her.

" Do you know," he said, " I heard that Mrs. Hallo, who
lives in Lemon Cottage, stole two of your balloons the other
day when you weren't looking."

With a leap the magic stick jerked itself off Tippy's arm,
and before the surprised pixie could get away it began to whip
him soundly again, crying out loudly all the time, " Tell-Tale
Tippy ! Tell-Tale Tippy ! "

In a trice a crowd collected, and, dear me, how delighted
everyone was to see Tippy being soundly whipped for telling
tales ! They clapped their hands and cheered, for there wasn't
a single person there that Tippy hadn't told tales about. Tippy
fought the stick, but it was too quick for him, and at last the
weeping pixie took to his heels and ran as fast as he could back

to his cottage. The magic stick flew after him and neatly hooked itself on to his arm again—and when at last the pixie got home he found that he had brought the stick with him!

"I'll punish you for beating me in front of everyone!" wept Tippy, angrily. "I'll burn you, see if I don't!"

He went out into the garden and made a big bonfire. Then he fetched the stick and threw it into the middle. The flames roared up and Tippy rubbed his hands in glee. Hurrah! Now the stick was done for!

He ran indoors to change his tunic, for he was to go to dinner with his Aunt Wumple, who lived at the other end of the village. He put on his best yellow silk tunic and his finest green knickerbockers. Then he sat down to read a book until it was time to go.

He didn't hear a tap-tap-tapping coming across the floor—but suddenly he felt something brushing against him—and, oh, my goodness me, it was the magic stick again! It wasn't burnt, but it had got all black and sooty in the fire, and when it brushed against Tippy's fine clothes it made them black and dirty.

"Go away, go away!" yelled Tippy, angrily. "I thought you were burnt! Look what a mess you have made of my clean clothes!"

The stick wouldn't go away. It wiped itself all up and down Tippy till it was clean—and you should have seen him when it had finished ! He was covered with sooty marks and looked a real little sweep !

He was ready to cry with rage. " All right ! " he said. " You wait, you miserable stick. I'll drown you ! "

He caught up the magic stick and ran to his well with it. Plonk ! Splash ! He threw it into the water far below and then left it there to drown.

" Ho ! " he thought, as he changed into some clean clothes, " that's the end of that nasty stick ! "

He hurried off to his Aunt Wumple's, and stayed with her until it was dark. Then he ran back home again, and undressed to go to bed, for it was late. He soon fell asleep, and began to snore.

Suddenly he woke with a jump ! Whatever was that noise ? He sat up. Something was squeezing itself in at the window, which was just a little bit open. Then, oh, dear me—tap-tap-tap, he heard across the wooden floor, and something crept close beside him under the bedclothes.

" Let me get close to you, I am cold and wet," said the voice of the magic stick. " I have struggled all the day to escape from the well, and I am tired and cold."

The wet stick pressed itself against Tippy, and he shivered. He got as far away from it as he could, but it crept after him. He didn't dare to push it away in case it began to whip him again. So all night long he and the magic stick lay shivering together, and Tippy was as scared a little pixie as you'd find anywhere.

In the morning he dressed very solemnly, and thought hard. He couldn't burn that stick—he couldn't drown it—perhaps he could chop it into pieces and use it for firewood. So he fetched his chopper, and laid the stick on the chopping-block. Chop ! Chop ! Chop ! It wasn't a bit of good, the stick was as hard as iron. Every time he chopped it it flew up and hit him on the nose, and soon Tippy threw down the chopper in despair.

"It's no good, Tippy," said the stick, hopping to the umbrella-stand. "You can't get rid of me. You must just put up with me, that's all."

So Tippy had to make up his mind to make the best of that magic stick. It went with him everywhere, and if he slipped out alone, it hopped after him and hooked itself on his arm. Every time he told a tale about someone the stick whipped him soundly and cried out loudly: "Tell-Tale Tippy! Tell-Tale Tippy!"

And soon Tippy thought twice before he told tales! If his tongue began to tell a tale, he felt the stick jerk on his arm, and he quickly made the tale a nice one, in case the stick should start to beat him again.

"Have you heard that Gobo——?" he would begin, and feel the stick jerk, ready to beat him if the tale was an unkind one—and quickly he would alter his tale. "Have you heard that Gobo gave a nice rocking-horse to the gardener's little boy? Wasn't it kind of him?"

Then the stick would rest quietly on his arm, and Tippy would be glad. But, dear me, how hard it was to remember to tell only nice things about his friends. For so many years he had been a nasty little tale-teller that he found it very difficult to stop. He had many a whipping before he learnt his lesson.

Then the day came when he knew that he would never, never tell tales again. He had grown to be a kind-hearted, generous little pixie, and although the magic stick still hung on to his arm whenever he went out, it no longer whipped him, for it never had any need to do so.

One morning, when Tippy was in the village shopping, the stick jerked itself off his arm, and went tap-tap-tapping down the street, all by itself.

" Where are you going ? " shouted Tippy.

" Oh, I'm off to seek my fortune ! " called back the stick.
" You do not need me now. You are no longer a tale-teller ! "

" Well, come back to me and be just an ordinary walking-stick ! " shouted Tippy. " I've grown quite fond of you, stick ! "

" No; no ! " called back the stick. " I am a magic stick.
I could never be an ordinary one. Good-bye, Tippy, don't
miss me too much. I'm off to find another tale-teller ! "

And with that it tapped away over the hill and was lost to
sight. It didn't go back to Too-Tall the Enchanter (who, you
will be glad to know, grew all his hair again through using his
Aunt Mickle-Muckle's hair-cream) and it never went back to
Tippy's village any more.

It is probably still tap-tap-tapping through the world, waiting
to hear someone tell an unkind tale about somebody else—
and then it will hook itself on to his arm, and wait until it can
give him a good beating ! So do be careful, won't you, not
to tell tales about anyone, because you never know when that
magic stick might be tap-tap-tapping somewhere near by!

The Snoozy Gnome

H AVE YOU heard of the Snoozy Gnome? His real name
was Tippit, but he was always called Snoozy. He was
the sleepiest, yawniest fellow that ever lived! He could
go to sleep at any time—even whilst running to catch a bus!

Now one day Snoozy's village was tremendously excited.
The Prince of Heyho was coming for the day, and so the
gnomes decided to give a fancy dress party in his honour.

" It shall be at five o'clock in the afternoon, so that even
the tiniest gnome can come," said Mister Big-Nose, the
chief gnome. " Now all go home, please, and think out some
really good fancy dresses for the party! "

Snoozy went home and sat down to think. ." I shall be a
bear! " he decided excitedly. " I can wear my bearskin rug,
and pull the head right over my head. I will pin it tightly
round me—and dear me, how astonished everyone will be!
That will be a fine fancy dress! "

When the day came, Snoozy took up his bearskin rug and
tried it on his back. He crawled about with the bear-head
over his head, and the rug over his back. He really looked
fine—just like a real bear!

" It's a bit big round my neck," thought Snoozy. " I must
alter that. Let me see—what is the time? Oh, only two
o'clock. I've got heaps of time till five."

He got out a big needle and a strong thread and sat down
to make the neck of the bearskin a little smaller. It was a hot
afternoon and Snoozy rested his head against a soft cushion.
He was very comfortable.

"Aaaaaah!" he yawned. "My goodness, I'd like a nap. I do feel sleepy!"

He looked at the clock again. "I think I'd have time just for ten minutes' snooze," he decided. "Then I shall be all fresh for the party!"

So he lay back and fell asleep. The time went on—three o'clock, four o'clock, five o'clock! And still Snoozy slept on! He dreamed pleasant dreams. He was as warm as toast, and his armchair was very comfortable. Oh, what a lovely snooze!

Time went on—six o'clock, seven o'clock, eight o'clock, nine o'clock. Snoozy, aren't you *ever* going to wake up? The party is over—everyone has gone home—and Mister Big-Nose is wondering why Snoozy didn't go to the party like everyone else!

Ten o'clock, eleven o'clock, midnight! The kitchen fire went out, and everywhere was quite dark and silent. Snoozy slept on, dreaming pleasantly. The clock ticked out the minutes in the darkness—but when the hands reached five minutes past four in the early morning, the clock stopped. It had to be wound up every night and as Snoozy had been asleep the evening before, it hadn't been wound up as usual.

After that there was no more ticking, and no more chiming. But the time went on—five o'clock, six o'clock, seven o'clock, eight o'clock! The sun was up, and most of the folk of the village. And at last Snoozy stirred in his armchair and stretched out his arms. He yawned widely—and opened his eyes. He looked round the room—and then he remembered the fancy dress party! My goodness!

" What's the time? " said Snoozy, and looked at the clock. " Five minutes past four! Gracious goodness, and the party is at five! I must hurry. I have had a longer snooze than I meant to have. Dear, dear, now I *shall* have a rush! "

You see, Snoozy hadn't any idea at all that he had slept all the night through. He simply thought he had slept till five minutes past four the day before—and he thought it was yesterday, not to-day! Poor old Snoozy! He didn't think of looking at the sun to see whereabouts in the sky it was, for, like most sleepy-headed people, he was rather stupid—and though the sun shone in at the wrong window, he still thought it was the afternoon!

" I shan't have time to alter the bearskin now," said Snoozy to himself. " Can't be bothered! My, how hungry I am! I shall eat quite twenty cakes at the party, and I believe I

could manage two or three jellies, and as for sausage-rolls, aha, give me fifteen of those, and you won't see them again!"

He put on the bearskin rug and pinned it tightly all round him. Then he pulled the bear-head over his own head, and pinned it well round his neck. He could hardly breathe, but he didn't mind. He was pleased to think he had such a fine fancy dress!

"Now, off we go!" said Snoozy and, crawling on all fours, he went out of his front door and down the street. As he went, he growled, because he thought that would make people look round and say: "Oh, look! Here's someone in a wonderful fancy dress!"

But the party was over long ago—and the folk of the village were hurrying to do their morning shopping. When they saw the life-like bear walking down the street, growling, they were frightened.

"Oh, oh!" they cried. "Look at that monster! He came out of Snoozy's house—he must have eaten him! Run, run!"

"Get a gun and shoot him!" cried Mister Big-Nose, meeting the bear round a corner, and getting the fright of his life.

Now Snoozy could NOT understand all this. So he stood up on his hind paws and shouted—or tried to shout through the bear-head: "I'm going to the party. Don't be frightened of me!"

But all that came out of the bear-head was something that sounded like : " Ah-wah-wah-wah-wah-wah-wah ! Wah-wah-wah-wah-wah-wah ! " It was really very difficult to speak with a big bear-head over his face, and Snoozy tried his best to talk clearly.

" Oh ! It's growling at us ! It's a *fierce* bear ! " shouted everyone in terror. " Listen to it jabbering ! "

Poor Snoozy was now quite puzzled. How stupid people were ! Couldn't they even *guess* that it was a fancy dress ? He shouted again, trying to say : " I tell you, I'm going to the fancy dress party ! Don't you UNDERSTAND ? "

But all that came out was something like : " Ah-who-wah, sh-wsh-wah-woo-wah-woowoowoo-wah ! Wah-woo—YAH-HAY-YAH ! "

" Oh ! It's getting fiercer ! " yelled the frightened people. " Mister Big-Nose, fetch a gun ! Oh, get a spear ! Oh, where's a great big stick to knock it on the head ! It'll eat us ! "

Snoozy was now quite frightened. A gun ! A spear ! A stick to knock him on the head ! Really, was everyone quite mad ? Wasn't he telling them he was going to the party ?

" I think I'd better go to the Town Hall, where the party is to be held, and then when people see me going up the steps, they will know I'm just someone in fancy dress," said Snoozy to himself. So he dropped down on all fours again and padded off to the Town Hall. Behind him came crowds of people, talking, pointing, and all ready to run away at once if the bear so much as turned his head.

But he didn't. He went right on to the Town Hall. He padded up the steps and into the big hall where three gnomes were busily sweeping up all the mess from the party the day before.

Snoozy stopped and looked in astonishment. " *Where* was the party ? " he wondered. " No tea—no balloons—no people there—no nothing ! "

He spoke to the three servants, who had been so busy with their work that they hadn't noticed the bear padding in. Snoozy said: "Where is the PARTY?"

But all the three servants heard was: "Wah-wah-wah-wah."

"Ooooooh!" they screeched in fright, when they saw the bear. "Oooooh! A wild bear! Growling at us! Chase him out, chase him out!"

So, to Snoozy's great surprise and anger, the three little gnomes rushed at him with big brooms and swept him out of the Town Hall! Yes, they really did, and it was very brave of them for they really and truly thought he was a wild bear from the woods.

"Don't! Don't!" yelled poor Snoozy. But as it sounded like "Woof! Woof!" it didn't help him much.

Bump, bumpity, bump-bump! Down the steps of the Town Hall went Snoozy, right to the very bottom. The three gnomes ran down after him and swept him into a very large puddle.

Snoozy was terribly upset. He sat in the puddle and. cried loudly : "Boo-hoo-hoo! Boo-hoo-hoo!"

And this time the noise he made was really like someone weeping, and all the

villagers stopped and looked at one another.

"The bear is crying!" they said. "The. bear is crying! Poor thing! Perhaps he has come with a message to someone. Ask him, Big-Nose!"

So Mister Big-Nose stepped forward and spoke to the bear. "Why have you come?" he said. "Do you want to speak to someone?"

"No," said Snoozy, and it sounded like "Woof!"

Big-Nose shook his head. "We can't understand what you say," he said.

Just then a small, sharp-eyed gnome gave a shout and pointed to the bear's neck. "He's got a safety-pin there!" he cried. "Do you think it is hurting him?"

"Where?" said Big-Nose, astonished. When he saw the safety-pin, he was very sorry for the bear. "Someone has put the pin there," he said. "Poor thing! Perhaps he came to ask us to get it out."

He undid the pin—and to his enormous surprise, the bear's head dropped sideways, and out of it came—Snoozy's own head, very hot, very rumpled, and with tears pouring down his cheeks!

"SNOOZY! It's SNOOZY!" cried everyone in the greatest astonishment. "What *are* you doing in a bearskin, Snoozy?"

"I c-c-came to the fancy dress p-p-party!" wept Snoozy. "But I couldn't find it."

"But that was *yesterday*, Snoozy!" said Big-Nose. "We wondered why you didn't come."

"Yesterday!" said Snoozy. "But I thought it was to be on Wednesday, not Tuesday."

"To-day is Thursday," said Big-Nose. "What *have* you been doing, Snoozy? Have you been asleep or something—and slept all round the clock? This is Thursday morning. What did you think it was?"

"Why, I thought it was Wednesday afternoon! And I came out dressed in my bearskin rug to go to the party. And now I've missed the party—and got swept down the

steps—and I'm bruised all over! Oh, why did I take that snooze! I must have slept all the afternoon and all the night—and my clock stopped at five past four, and I thought that was the real time!"

Everyone began to laugh. It was really such a joke. "Snoozy came to the party the day after!" said one gnome to another. "Poor old Snoozy! What *will* he do next! And he was swept down the steps, too! Ho, ho! Perhaps he won't be quite so snoozy next time!"

Snoozy went home, carrying the bearskin over his shoulder. He was very unhappy. He got himself some bread and jam, for he was very hungry, and then he sat down to eat it. But so many tears ran down his nose into the jam that they made it taste quite salty, and he didn't enjoy his breakfast at all.

"That's the last time I snooze!" said the gnome. "Never again!"

But it takes more than one lesson to cure a snoozer. Before a week was out, Snoozy was napping again—what a sleepyhead he is!

The Three Strange Travellers

ONCE upon a time there was a billy-goat who drew a little goat-carriage on the sea-sands. He took children quite a long ride for a penny. But one day, when he was getting old, he became lame. He limped with his right front foot, and he could no longer draw the goat-carriage along at a fine pace.

" You are no use to me now," said his master, a cross and selfish old man. " I shall buy a new goat."

The old billy-goat bleated sadly. What would he do if his master no longer needed him ?

" You can go loose on the common," said the old man. " Don't come to me for a home, for I don't want you any longer."

Poor Billy-goat ! He was very unhappy. He looked at his little goat-carriage for the last time, and then he limped off to the common. The winter was coming on, and he hoped he would not freeze to death. He had always lived in a cosy shed in the winter-time—but now he would have no home.

He hadn't gone very far across the common when he heard a loud quacking behind him.

" Quack ! Stop, I say ! Hey, stop a minute ! Quack ! "

Billy-goat turned round. He saw a duck waddling along as fast as it could, quacking loudly.

" Whats' the matter ? " asked Billy.

" Matter enough ! " said the duck, quite out of breath. " Do you mind if I walk with you ? There are people after me who will kill me if they find me."

" Mercy on us ! " said the goat, startled. " Why do they want to kill you ? "

"Well," said the duck indignantly, "I don't lay as many eggs as I did, and my master says I'm no use now, so he wants to eat me for his dinner. And I have served him well for many many months, laying delicious eggs, far nicer than any hen's!"

"Dear me," said Billy-goat, "you and I seem to have the same kind of master. Maybe they are brothers. Well, Duck, walk with me. I am seeking my fortune, and would be glad of company."

The two walked on together, the goat limping and the duck waddling. When they reached the end of the common they came to a farm.

"Do not go too near," said the duck. "I don't wish to be caught. Do you?"

"No," said the goat. "Listen! What's that?"

They stood still and heard a great barking. Suddenly a little dog squeezed itself under a near-by gate and came running towards them. The duck got behind the goat in fright, and the goat stood with his horns lowered in case the dog should attack him.

"Don't be afraid of me," panted the dog. "I am running away. My master has beaten me because I let a fox get two chickens last night. But what could I do? I was chained up and I could not get at the fox. I barked loudly, but my master was too fast asleep to hear me. And now he blames me for the fox's theft!"

"You are to be pitied," said the goat. "We too have had bad masters. Come with us, and we will keep together and look after ourselves. Maybe we shall find better masters."

"I will come," said the dog. "I am getting old, you know, and I cannot see as well as I used to do. I think my master wants to get rid of me and have a younger dog. Ah me, there is no kindness in the world these days!"

The three animals journeyed on together. They ate what

they could find. The billy-goat munched the green grass, the duck swam on each pond she came to and hunted about for food in the mud at the bottom. The dog sometimes found a bit of bread or a hunk of meat thrown by the wayside.

They walked for miles and miles. Often the goat and the dog gave the duck rides on their backs, for she waddled so slowly, and soon got tired. At night they found a sheltered place beneath a bush, or beside a haystack, and slept there in a heap, the duck safely in the middle.

They became very fond of one another, and vowed that they would never separate. But as the days grew colder the three creatures became anxious.

" When the ponds are frozen I shall find no food," said the duck.

"And I shall not be able to eat grass when the ground is covered with snow," said the goat. "I shall freeze to death at night, for I have always been used to a shed in the winter."

"And I have been used to a warm kennel," said the dog. "What shall we do?"

They could think of no plan, so they wandered on. Then one afternoon a great storm blew up. Oh, my, what a wind! The snow came down softly everywhere, but the blizzard was so strong that even the soft snowflakes stung the dog's eyes and made the duck and the goat blink.

"We shall be lost altogether in this dreadful storm!" barked the dog. "We must find shelter."

The goat and the duck followed him. He put his nose to the ground and ran off. He went up a little hill, and at last came to a small cottage. There was a light in one of the windows.

"Somebody lives here," said the dog. "Let us knock at the door and ask for shelter."

So the goat tapped the door with his hoof. He bleated as he did so, the dog whined, and the duck quacked.

Inside the cottage was an old woman with a red shawl round her shoulders. She was darning a hole in a stocking and thinking about the dreadful storm. Suddenly she heard the tap-tap-tapping at her door.

"Bless us!" she cried, in a fright. "There's someone there! Shall I open the door or not? It may be a robber come through the storm to rob me of the gold pieces I have hidden so carefully in my old stocking under the mattress! No, I dare not open the door!"

As she sat trembling she heard the dog whining. Then she heard the bleating of the goat and the anxious quacking of the duck.

"Well, well!" she said in astonishment. "It sounds for all the world like a dog, a goat, and a duck! But how do they come to my door like this? Do they need shelter from this

terrible storm, poor things ? Well, I have no shed to put them in, so they must come in here with me."

She got up and went to the door. She undid the bolt and opened the door a crack. When she saw the trembling goat, the shivering dog, and the frightened duck, her kind heart melted at once and she opened the door wide.

" Poor lost creatures ! " she said. " Come in, come in. You shall have warmth and shelter whilst this storm lasts. Then I've no doubt you will want to go back to your homes."

The three animals gladly came in to the warmth. The dog at once lay down on the hearth-rug, the goat stood near by, and the duck lay down in a corner, put her head under her wing and fell fast asleep, for she was very tired.

The old woman didn't know what to make of the three creatures. They seemed to know one another so well, and by the way they bleated, barked, and quacked to one another they could talk as well as she could.

The goat was very thin, and the dog was skinny too. As for the duck, when the old woman felt her, she was nothing but feathers and bone !

" The poor creatures ! " said the kind old dame. " They are starving ! I will give them a good meal to eat—they will feel all the better for it."

So she began to cook a meal of all the household scraps she had—bits of meat, vegetables, potatoes, bread, all sorts. How good it smelt! Even the duck in the corner stuck out her head from under her wing to have a good sniff.

The old woman took the big saucepan off the fire and stood it on the window-sill to cool. Then she ladled the warm food out into three dishes and put one in front of each animal.

"There, my dears," she said, "eat that and be happy to-night."

Well, the three animals could hardly believe their eyes to see such a feast! They gobbled up the food and left not a single scrap. Then the goat rubbed his head gently against the old dame's knee, the dog licked her hand, and the duck laid its head on her shoe. Then they all curled up in a heap together, and fell asleep. The old dame went to her bed and slept too.

In the morning the storm was over, but the countryside was covered with snow. The animals did not want to leave the warm cottage, but the old woman opened the door.

"Now you must find your way home," she said. She did not know that they had no homes. She thought they had lost their way in the storm, and that now they would be glad to go out and find their way back to their homes.

The animals were sad. They took leave of the kind woman, and wished they could tell her that they would like to stay ; but she could not understand their language. They went out into the snow, and wondered where to go next.

"Let us go down the hill," said the goat. "See, there are some haystacks, and we may be able to find some food and shelter under the stacks to-night."

So down the hill they went. But they could not find any food. They crouched under the haystack that evening, and tried to get warm. As they lay there, quite still, they heard the sound of soft footsteps in the snow. Then they heard voices.

" The old woman has a great hoard of gold," said one voice.
" We will go to her cottage to-night, when she is in bed, and
steal it."

" Very well," said the second voice. " I will meet you there,
and we will share the gold. She has no dog to bark or bite."

The animals listened in horror. Why, it must be the kind
old woman these horrid men were speaking of ! How could
they save her from the robbers ?

" We must go back to the cottage," said the dog. " Somehow we must creep in and wait for these robbers. Then we
will set on them and give them the fright of their lives ! "

So the three limped, walked, and waddled all the way up
the hill until they came to the little cottage. The old woman
was going to bed. The goat peeped in at the window and saw
her blow her candle out.

" She has left this window a little bit open," he said to the
dog. " Can you jump in and open the door for me and the
duck ? "

" Yes," said the dog, " I can do that. I often saw my
master open the farm doors. I know how to do it."

He squeezed in through the window and went to the door.
He pulled at the latch. The door was not bolted, so the goat
and the duck came in at once. They could hear the old dame
snoring.

" What shall we do when the robbers come ? " asked the
duck excitedly.

" I have a plan," said the goat. " You, duck, shall first of all
frighten the robbers by quacking at the top of your very loud
voice. You, dog, shall fly at the legs of the first robber, and
I will lower my head and butt the second one right in the middle.
Ha ! what a fright we will give them ! "

The three animals were so excited that they could hardly
keep still. The duck flew up on the table and stood there.
The dog hid behind the door. The goat stood ready on the

hearth-rug, for he wanted a good run when he butted the
second robber.

Presently the dog's sharp ears told him that the two robbers
were outside. He warned the others and they got ready to do
their parts. The robbers pushed the door open.

At that moment the duck opened her beak and quacked.
How she quacked! QUACK! QUACK! QUACK! QUACK!
QUACK!

Then the dog flew at the legs of the first robber and bit
them. And he growled. GRRRRRRRRRRRRR! What a terrible
growl it was!

Then the goat ran at the second robber and butted him so
hard in the middle that he sat down suddenly and lost all his
breath.

The duck was so excited that she wanted to join in the fun.
So she flew to the robbers and pecked their noses hard. PECK!
PECK!

The robbers were frightened almost out of their lives. They
couldn't think what was happening! There was such a terrible
noise going on, and something was biting, hitting, and peck-
ing them from top to toe. How they wished they had never
come near the cottage!

As soon as they could they got to their feet and ran. The
duck flew after them and pecked their ankles. The dog tore

pieces out of their trousers. The goat limped as fast as he could and butted them down the hill. My, what a set-to it was!

The two robbers fell into a ditch and covered themselves with mud.

"That old woman is a witch!" cried one.

"Yes, she pinched my ears!" said the other. "And she bit my legs!"

"Ho, and she punched me in the middle so that I lost all my breath!" said the first.

"And all the time she made such a noise!" cried the second, trying to clamber out of the ditch. "She said: 'Whack! Whack! Whack!'"

"Yes, and she cried: 'Cuff! Cuff! Cuff!' too!" said the first. "And how she chased us down the hill!"

The three animals laughed till the tears came into their eyes when they heard the robbers talking like this.

"They thought my 'Quack, quack, quack!' was 'Whack, whack, whack!'" said the duck in delight.

"And they thought my 'Wuff, wuff, wuff!' was 'Cuff, cuff, cuff!'" said the dog, jumping about joyfully. "What a joke! How we frightened them!"

"Let us go back and see if the old dame is all right," said the goat. "She woke when the duck began to quack."

Back they all went to the cottage, and found the old dame sitting up in bed, trembling, with a candle lighted by her side. When she saw the three animals she could hardly believe her eyes.

"So it was you who set upon those robbers and chased them away!" she said. "You dear, kind, clever creatures! Why, I thought you had gone to your homes!"

The goat went up to the bed and put his front paws there. The dog put his nose on the quilt. The duck flew up on the bed-rail and flapped her wings.

"Wuff!" said the dog, meaning: "We want to stay with you!"

"Bleat!" said the goat, and meant the same thing.

"Quack!" said the duck, and she meant the same thing too.

And this time the old dame understood them, and she smiled joyfully.

"So you want to stay here?" she said. "Well, you shall. I'm all alone and I want company. It's wintertime and I expect you need shelter, so you shall all live with me. I shall always be grateful to you for chasing away those robbers."

Well, those three animals soon settled down with the old woman. The duck laid an egg for her breakfast each day. The dog lay on the door-mat and guarded the cottage for her each night. The goat was troubled because he could do nothing for his kind mistress.

But one day he found how well he could help her. She had to go to the woods to get firewood. She took with her a little cart to bring it back, and this she had to pull herself, for she had no pony.

But the goat stood himself in the shafts and bleated. The old woman saw that he wanted her to tie the cart to him so that he might pull the wood home for her, and she was delighted. Every day after that the goat took the cart to the woods for his mistress, and very happy they were together.

As for the robbers, they have never dared to come back. They went a hundred miles away, and told the people there a marvellous story of an old witch who cried : " Whack ! Cuff ! Whack ! Cuff ! " and could bite, pinch, and punch all at once. But nobody believed them.

The old dame and the dog, goat, and duck still live together very happily. Their house is called " Windy Cottage," so if ever you pass by, go in and see them all. The old dame will love to tell you the story of how they came to live together !

c

She Turned Up Her Nose

IN THE nursery there lived a rather grand doll called Anna-bella Mary. She was dressed very well indeed in a blue silk frock, a hat with flowers in, shoes with blue bows on, and a very pretty white lace coat.

She thought herself a very grand person, and turned up her nose at all the other toys. She wouldn't join in their games. She wouldn't play with the golliwog because she said he ought to wash himself, and get himself white. She wouldn't even have a ride in the little toy car.

One day the small dolls who lived in the dolls' house thought they would spring-clean it and make it beautifully clean and pretty. The children who belonged to the nursery were away, so it was a good chance to spring-clean the dolls' house.

" We'll all help," said the golliwog. " I'll scrub the floors."

" I'll clean the windows," said the Teddy.

" I'll beat the mats," said Angela, the golden-haired doll.

" I'll wash the curtains," said the clockwork mouse. But it was a great pity the toys allowed him to do that, because he tore the lace curtains badly, and four of them couldn't possibly be put up again.

" Oh dear ! " said the dolls' house dolls, sadly, looking at the great holes in four of their curtains. " Oh dear ! What a pity ! The four bedroom windows will look awful now, without any curtains. Never mind, don't cry, clockwork mouse—you did your best. It was our fault for letting a little thing like you wash the curtains."

Soon the house was as clean and bright as a new pin. The floors shone. The carpets were beaten and put down again.

The windows were clean. The fire-places had been swept out. The furniture had been polished, and the cushions beaten free of dust. Really, the house looked lovely.

"I think we ought to give a party to everyone," said the dolls' house Mother-doll. "They've been so kind in helping us to spring-clean."

"We won't ask Annabella Mary, the stuck-up doll," said the dolls' house Father-doll. "She hasn't helped at all. She just sat in her chair in a corner of the nursery, in her grand coat, and turned up her nose at us all working so busily **at** getting the house clean. We won't ask *her*!"

"Indeed we won't!" said all the others. So they didn't. Annabella Mary was the only toy who didn't get an invitation card to the party.

She didn't know anything about it until she saw the others reading their party-cards. She went over to the golliwog and peeped over his shoulder.

"Ha!" she said, pleased. "An invitation to a party in the dolls' house! What fun! I love parties."

"You're not going to be asked," said the golliwog. "You haven't got an invitation card, have you? You see—you didn't help at all when we were so busy—so the dolls' house dolls didn't see why you should share in the fun afterwards. Quite right, too. You always turn your nose up at everything and everyone, so we are just as pleased you won't be going. You'd turn your nose up at the little cakes. You'd turn your nose up at the little cups of sweet lemonade. Oh, it's a good thing you're not going."

Now, it is a very horrid thing to be left out of anything nice, and Annabella Mary didn't like it at all. At first she was angry, and pretended to turn up her nose at the party. "What a silly party it will be!" she said loudly. "I'm sure *I* wouldn't want to go to it!"

But after a bit, when she saw how excited everyone was getting, and heard all about the little cakes and biscuits that were being made on the stove in the dolls' house, she felt very sad.

"Am I really so horrid?" she thought. "Do I really turn my nose up at things and make people dislike me? It isn't nice not to be liked. I wish I'd helped to clean the dolls' house now. I could have taken off my grand coat and frock, and worn an overall. I wish I hadn't been so mean. It serves me right to be left out!"

Annabella
Mary felt
sadder and
sadder when
the time drew
near for the
party. She
stood by the
dolls' house,
and watched
what was
going on.

"I *do* wish
the clockwork mouse hadn't torn the curtains for the four
bedroom windows," she heard the Mother-doll say with a
sigh. "The house looks so sweet—but the bedroom windows
look empty and bare."

Annabella Mary looked at the windows. They certainly
did look bare without their little lace curtains. As she stared
at them an idea came into her mind. What about her grand
lace coat? Couldn't she cut it up into four bits, hem the ends,
and make four little curtains for the windows?

"Oh, if only I could!" said Annabella Mary. "That
would show the toys I'm not so mean, after all. I'll do it!"

So, whilst the others were all busy getting ready for the
party, Annabella cut up the lace coat she was so proud of
and sewed the four pieces neatly into little lace curtains.
Then, much to the surprise of all the toys, she hung them up
at the bedroom windows of the dolls' house. She was tall
enough to reach the window without going inside the house.
She opened each tiny window, and hung the curtain across.

"Look what Annabella Mary's doing!" cried the toys.
"Where did she get the lace?"

"Oh, she's cut up her beautiful lace coat, the one she's so

proud of!" cried the golly. "Annabella Mary, why did you do that?"

"Well, I hadn't done anything to help, you see," said the big doll. "And I suddenly thought of this. I've been mean and horrid, always turning up my nose—but now I feel different."

"Oh, Annabella, the curtains are SIMPLY LOVELY!" cried the dolls' house dolls. "All they want is little bows of ribbon now!"

"Here they are!" cried Annabella, and snipped the blue bows off her shoes! She pinned them to the curtains—and, dear me, how fine the bedroom windows looked!

"You must come to the party, you really must," said the golly. "Why, you are a really nice person, after all. We shall have fun with you. Come and join the party. See if you like our cakes."

So Annabella joined the party, and instead of turning up her nose at everything, and saying it wasn't nice, she said everything was lovely, and that it was the best party she had ever been to. It was, too, because, for the first time, she made real friends with everyone, and was as happy as could be.

The little bedroom curtains are still there, with tiny blue bows on them. I do wish you could see them!

The Secret Cave

THE adventure of the Secret Cave really began on the day when we all went out on the cliff to fly our new kite. I am Roger, and Joan and William are my sister and brother. William's the eldest, and Joan and I are twins.

We live in a house near the sea, but it is very lonely because there is no other house anywhere near us, except the big house on the cliff, and that is empty. We often wished it was full of children so that we could play with them, but as it wasn't we had to be content to play by ourselves.

Mummy and Daddy were going away for a month on a sea-trip, and they were leaving that very day. We were all feeling very sad about it, because home is a funny sort of place without Mummy. But it was holiday time, and our governess had gone, so there was only old Sarah to look after us, and we thought we'd have quite a good time really.

Mummy gave us a glorious new kite just as she said good-bye, and told us to go and fly it as soon as they had gone; then we shouldn't feel so bad about everything. So when the car had disappeared down the hill, we took our new kite and went out on the windy cliff.

William soon got it up in the air, and it flew like a bird. But suddenly the wind dropped and the kite gave a great dip downwards. William pulled hard at it, but it wasn't any good. Down and down it went, and at last disappeared behind some trees.

" Bother ! " we said. " Let's go and look for it."

We raced over the cliff till we came to the clump of stunted trees behind which our kite had gone. Then we found that the string disappeared over the high wall that surrounded the big house on the cliff.

" The kite must have fallen in the garden," said William. " What shall we do ? "

" Go and knock at the front door and ask for it," said Joan. "There might be a caretaker there."

So we ran

round to the front gate and went up the long drive. We soon came to the front door. It was a big wooden one with a large knocker. William knocked hard and we heard the sound go echoing through the house.

Nobody came, so we each of us knocked in turn, very loudly indeed. After we had waited for about five minutes without anyone opening the door, we decided that the house must be quite empty, without a caretaker or anyone at all.

" Well, how are we to get our kite ? " I asked.

" The only thing to do is to climb over the wall," said William. " We can't ask anyone's permission because there isn't anyone to ask. Come on. We can't lose our lovely kite."

So we ran down the drive again and made our way to the back of the garden wall, which stood high above our heads. William managed to climb up it first, and then jumped down on the other side.

"Come on, you others," he called. "It's all right. Oh, wait a minute, though. I've got an idea. Stand away from the wall, both of you. I've found a box here, and I'm going to throw it over. You can stand on it, and then you will easily be able to climb up the wall."

William threw over the box. Then we stood on it and just managed to reach the top. We jumped down, and there we all were in the deserted garden of the house on the cliff.

It was a very wild place, for no one had bothered about it for years. Everything was overgrown, and the paths were covered with green moss that was like velvet to walk on. I don't know why, but we felt at first as if we ought to talk in whispers.

"Where's our kite?" said Joan. "Look, William, there's the string. Let's follow it and we shall soon find the kite."

So we followed the string, and it led us over a stretch of long grass that had once been a big lawn, down a thick shrubbery, and past some greenhouses whose glass was all broken.

Then William gave a shout.

"There it is!" he said, and he pointed to where a little shed stood hidden away in a dark corner. We all looked at it, and, sure enough, there was the kite perched up on the roof. It didn't take us long to pull it down, and we found that one of the sticks that ran across it was broken, so we couldn't fly it any more that day. We were sorry about that, and we wondered what we should do for the rest of the morning.

"Why can't we stay here and explore the garden?" asked Joan. "We shouldn't do any harm, and it would be great fun."

"All right, we will," said William, who always decides everything because he is the eldest.

So we began exploring, and it really was fun. Then it suddenly began to rain, and as we none of us had our mackintoshes with us we got wet.

"We must shelter somewhere," said William. "Sarah will be very cross if we go home soaked through."

" Well, what about that little shed, where we found the kite ? " I asked. " That would do nicely."

So we raced to the shed, but the door was locked, so we couldn't get in.

" How about a window ? " cried Joan. " Here's one with the latch broken. Push it, William. Oh, good, it's open and we can climb in. What an adventure we're having ! "

We all climbed in. I went to the door, and what do you think ? The key was *inside* !

" Well, if that isn't a curious thing," said William, looking at it. " If you lock a door from the inside you usually lock yourself in too. But there's nobody here. It's a mystery ! "

But we soon forgot about the key in our excitement over the shed. It really was a lovely little place. There was a funny old chair with a crooked leg that William felt sure he could mend if he had his tools. There was a battered old table in one corner, and two small stools, one with a leg off. Along one side of the shed was a shelf, very dusty and dirty.

" I say ! Wouldn't this shed make a perfectly lovely little house for us to play in on rainy days ? " suddenly said William. " We could clean it up and mend the stool and chair."

" Oh, William, do let's ! " said Joan, clapping her hands in delight. " I've got some pretty orange stuff Mummy gave me, and I can make it into little curtains for the two windows. We can bring a pail and a scrubbing-brush and clean the whole place up beautifully."

" And we can use the shelf for storing things on," I said. " We can bring apples and biscuits here, and some of our books to read. Oh, what fun ! But we must keep it a secret, or perhaps Sarah would stop us."

" Well, we mustn't do any harm anywhere," said William. " After all, it isn't *our* shed, but I'm sure if the man who owns it, whoever he is, knew that we were going to clean it up and make it nice, he would only be too glad to let us. Now the

rain's stopped
—we must
run home or
we shall be
late for din-
ner."

We took
our broken
kite and
raced home.
We didn't
need to climb
over the wall
again, because
we found a
dear little
door in the
wall with the

key inside. So we opened the door, slipped out, locked it
again, and William took the key away in his pocket in case
tramps found it.

We were so excited at dinner-time that Sarah got cross with
us and threatened to send us to bed half an hour earlier if we
didn't eat our food properly.

At last dinner was over and we ran out into our own garden
to decide what we should take to the house on the cliff.

"Let's borrow the gardener's barrow," said William.
"We can put heaps of things in that and wheel it easily."

So we got the barrow and piled the things into it. Joan
found the orange stuff and put that in, and popped her work-
basket in too. I found a very old carpet that nobody used
in the attic, and I put that in. William took his tools, and we
went and asked Cook if she could give us anything to eat.

She was very nice, and gave us three slices of cake, a bottle of lemonade, and a bag of raisins. Then we had a great stroke of luck, because the gardener told us we could pick the apples off one of the trees and keep them for ourselves.

You can guess we had soon picked about fifty or sixty and put them into a basket. That went into the barrow too, and then it really was almost as much as we could manage to wheel it along.

"We can easily come back for our books and anything else we can think of," said William. So off we went, all helping to push. At last we came to the little door in the wall and William unlocked it. We went through the garden until we came to our dear little shed.

"Oh, we ought to have brought something to clean it up with," said Joan. "Never mind, William. Empty these things out on to a newspaper in the corner, and we'll go back for a pail and a scrubbing-brush and soap."

Back we went, and at last after two or three more journeys we really had got everything we could think of that day. Then we had a lovely time cleaning up the shed. The floor was laid with big white flagstones, and they looked lovely when we had scrubbed them clean. We washed the shelf and all the bits of furniture too, and soon the shed looked fine.

That was all we had time to do that day, but early the next morning we were back again, as you can guess. Joan made the little curtains and tied them back with a piece of old hair-ribbon. They did look nice. William and I mended the stool and the chair and arranged the things we had brought.

Cook had given us half a jar of strawberry jam and a pot of honey, and we had bought some biscuits and nuts. Our books went up on the shelf, and the apples stood in a corner in their basket.

"Well, it really looks quite homey," said Joan, jumping round the shed joyfully. "What fun we shall have here. Don't my little curtains look nice, and isn't the carpet fine? Our feet would have been very cold on those bare flagstones."

Well, I can't tell you how we enjoyed our time in that little shed. Every day that it rained we went there, and as it was a very wet summer we spent most of our time there. We ate our biscuits and apples, read our books and did puzzles, and Sarah thought we were as good as gold, though she didn't know at all where we went every day. She thought we were down by the sea, I think.

But the most exciting part of our adventure hadn't come yet. I must tell you about it now.

We had been using the shed for about three weeks when William lost a sixpence. It rolled on to the floor and disappeared. We turned back the carpet to look for it.

" There's a flagstone here that seems rather loose," said William. " Perhaps the sixpence has gone down the crack."

" It *is* loose ! " said Joan. "Why, I can almost lift it ! "

" I believe we *could* lift it," said William. We slipped a thin iron bar in one of the cracks, and then suddenly the stone rose up ! It came quite easily, and stood upright, balanced on one side.

And where it had been was a big black hole, with stone steps leading downwards!

What do you think of that ? We were all so astonished that we simply knelt there and stared and stared.

" Why, it's a

secret passage!" said William at last. "What about exploring it?"

"Do you think it's safe?" asked Joan.

"Oh, I should think so," said William. "We can take our electric torches with us. This passage explains the key left inside the door. Someone must have gone to this shed, locked it from the inside, and then gone down the passage somewhere. It must lead out to some place or other. Oh, what an adventure!"

We got our torches from the shelf, and then, with William leading, we all climbed down the steps. They soon ended and we found ourselves in a narrow passage that led downwards fairly steeply.

"Do you know, I believe this passage leads to the seashore," said William suddenly. "I think it is going right through the cliff, and will come out to one of those rocky caves we have sometimes seen from a boat."

And we found that

William was right. For the passage, always sloping down-wards, suddenly opened out into a small dark cave. William couldn't see at first whether or not there was any way out of it besides the way we had come, and then he suddenly found it! It was just a small opening low down at one end, so small that a man would have found it quite difficult to squeeze through.

We squeezed through easily enough, of course, and then we found ourselves in a very big wide cave, lit by daylight. The thunder of breaking waves seemed very near, and as we made our way to the big opening where the daylight streamed through we saw the rough sea just outside it.

"You were right, William," I said. "That passage from our shed led right through the cliff down to this cave that is open to the sea. Look! When we stand on this ledge the waves almost reach our feet. I shouldn't be surprised if in very rough weather the sea washes right into the cave."

"I don't think so," said William, turning round to look. "You see, the floor slopes upwards fairly steeply. Oh my! Just look there!"

We turned to see what he was exclaiming at, and what do you think? The floor of the cave was strewn with boxes of all sizes and shapes!

"Why, perhaps it's a smugglers' cave!" we cried. We rushed to the boxes, but all except two were fast locked. In the two unlocked ones were many clothes—very old-fashioned ones they were, too.

"Well, this *is* a find!" said William. "I say, what about dressing up in these clothes and giving Sarah a surprise?"

We thought that would be lovely, so we quickly turned out the clothes and found some to fit us. Joan had a lovely frock right down to her ankles, and I had a funny little tunic sort of suit, and so did William. We put them on in the little shed because it was lighter there.

"Now, are we all ready?" said William. "Well, come

along then. We'll give Sarah the surprise of her life, and then we'll take her and the gardener to see our wonderful find."

We danced through the door of the shed—and oh, my gracious goodness, didn't we get a shock?

Two gentlemen were walking up the moss-grown path by the shed! They saw us just at the same moment as we saw them, and we all stopped quite still and stared at one another.

One of the gentlemen looked as if he simply couldn't believe his eyes   He took off his glasses and cleaned them, and

then he put them on again. But we were still there, and at last he spoke to us.

"Am I dreaming—or am I back in the days of long ago?" he said. "Are you children of nowadays, or little long-ago ghosts?"

"We're quite real," said William. "We're only dressed up."

"Well, that's a relief," said the man. "But what are you doing here? This garden belongs to my house."

"Oh, are you the man who owns the house?" asked William.

"Yes," he answered, "and this gentleman is perhaps going to buy it from me. I'm too poor to keep it as it should be kept, you see. But you still haven't told me what you are doing here."

Well, of course, we had to confess everything then. We told him how we had found the dear little shed by accident, and made it a sort of a home. And then we told him of our great find that afternoon.

"What!" he cried. "Do you really mean to say you've found the secret passage to the cave? Why, it's been lost for years and years, and no one knew the secret. I lived here when I was a boy, but I never found it either, though I looked everywhere."

Of course we had to show the way down to the cave, and when he saw the boxes lying there he turned so pale that Joan asked him if he was going to faint.

" No," he said. " But I'm going to tell you a little story, and you will understand then why I feel rather queer."

And this is the story he told us.

" Many, many years ago," he began, " my family lived in France. There came a time when they were unjustly accused as traitors, and were forced to fly from the country. They packed up all their belongings and put them on board a ship to be brought to this country, where they had a house. This was the house. It had a secret passage from the shed to the sea, and the idea was to land at night with their belongings and go up through the passage unseen. They meant to live in the house until the trouble had blown over and they could go about here in safety, or return to France."

" And did they ? " asked William.

" No. Just as all the luggage had been safely put on board and the family were saying good-bye to their friends on shore, some men came galloping up and took them prisoners. The ship hurriedly put off without them and sailed safely to this place. The luggage was dumped down in this cave and the ship went back towards France. But, so the story goes, a storm came, and the whole crew were drowned. As for the family, some died in prison, and none of them ever came back to this house except one. He had been a small boy at the time and had no idea where the secret passage was, and though he searched everywhere he could not find it. So he gave it up and decided that all the family belongings were lost for ever."

" And are these what he was looking for ? " I asked.

" They are," said the man. " And, thanks to you, they are found again. Well, well, what an excitement ! Now perhaps

I shan't have to sell my own house. I might even be able to come and live here again with my family."

" Have you got any children ? " asked William.

" Yes, six," said the man.

Well, we all gave a shout at that ! Fancy having six children near to play with, when you've never had any at all ! It seemed too good to be true.

But it *was* true ! Mr. Carnot, for that was the man's name, found that the boxes did contain all his old family treasures, and by selling some he had more than enough money to live at his old home once again with his family. I can tell you it was a most exciting day when they all arrived.

Daddy and Mummy could hardly believe all we had to tell them when they came home, but when Mr. Carnot took them into our shed and down the passage to the cave, they soon knew it was true.

And now we have heaps of playmates. They are Billy, Anne, Marjorie, Jeanne, Laurence, and the baby. We often use the secret passage, and sometimes we even row to the cave in a boat, just like the sailors did all those many years ago.

The Proud Little Dog

THERE was once a dog called Prince, and he lived with Dame Tiptap. She was very proud of him when he first came to her as a puppy, because his father and mother and his two grandmothers and two grandfathers had all won prizes.

Dame Tiptap gave Prince a beautiful basket of his own, lined with red flannel to keep him warm. She bought him a very expensive collar. She went to a pottery and had a special dish made for him, with his name " Prince " round the bowl.

Prince thought himself very grand indeed. He looked at the old dog kennel out in the yard, and thought to himself, " Ha! That may be good enough for ordinary dogs, but a dog like me sleeps by the fire, in a red-lined basket! I'm a prince among dogs! "

So, as he grew, he became very vain and proud. He looked down on the other dogs. He would not have a cat in the garden. He even chased away the birds that came for crumbs!

" Any crumbs in this garden belong to *me*! " said Prince.

" Fibber! They are put out for us! " chirruped the sparrow on the roof. " Besides—what do *you* want with crumbs? Don't you have a big dinner? "

Prince did not like his mistress to have friends to the house. He growled at them. He even showed his teeth. Dame Tiptap did not like it.

She scolded him. " This won't do, Prince. If you behave like that to my friends, I shall put you out into the kitchen when they come! "

"If you do a thing like that, I'll run away!" growled Prince, rudely.

"The trouble is, you're spoilt," said Dame Tiptap. "Now just you listen to me. Mistress Twinkle is coming to tea to-day. If you dare to bark or growl or show your teeth—out into the kitchen you go!"

Well, Prince *did* bark—and he did growl—and he did show his teeth! So out into the kitchen he went, and the door was shut firmly. He was very angry indeed, especially as he could smell muffins toasting in the sitting-room, and he liked them very much.

"I won't be treated like this!" growled Prince crossly. "I shall run away! That will teach Dame Tiptap her manners. She'll miss me. She'll have no one to guard the house. Ha, ha!"

He ran out of the back-door, down the path and away into the fields. He was a very good-looking dog, and he held up his head and kept his tail well up as he went. It was no wonder that a passing tramp looked at him closely and thought he would be a fine dog to steal !

" He's a valuable dog, anyone can see that," said the tramp, and he whistled to Prince. Prince ran up at once—and in a trice the man had slipped some rope through his collar and was leading him away.

" I'll tie him up for a few days and then sell him," thought the tramp. " Now come on, dog—don't drag behind like that. What—you won't come ! Well, I've a stick here. How do you like it ? Whack, whack, whack ! Ah, now you'll come along all right ! "

Poor Prince. He was taken to the man's tumble-down cottage and tied up tightly at the back. He was frightened and unhappy.

Dame Tiptap did not know where he had gone. " Foolish dog ! " she said. " He has run away, as he said. Well, if he cares so little for his home and mistress, it is not much use worrying about him. Now I can have a cat of my own. I never dared to have one before. I'll tell Mistress Twinkle I will take the lovely black cat she has offered me—the one with eyes as green as cucumbers. She's a beauty, and will catch my mice for me."

So the next day Green-Eyes came to live with kind Dame Tiptap. She settled down in Prince's basket by the fire, delighted to find such a good home. At night she hunted mice, and Dame Tiptap was very pleased with her.

Then somebody gave Dame Tiptap a canary in a cage, to sing to her in the mornings. She hung it up in the window, and told Green-Eyes never to jump at the cage. It was lovely to hear the little bird singing every morning.

A week went by—and one morning, what a surprise for Dame Tiptap ! In Green-Eyes' basket were four beautiful kittens, all with eyes fast shut. But they were not asleep. New-born kittens always have their eyes shut at first.

"Well, well, look at that now!" said Dame Tiptap, delighted. "I've always loved kittens. Now we've got four! What fun we shall have when they run about!"

Now after some time Prince bit through the rope that tied him, and ran home as fast as ever he could. He had had very little food. He had a cold. He was homesick and miserable. How he looked forward to his warm basket by the fire, a good dinner in the dish marked with his own name, and a great fussing from Dame Tiptap! He ran through the back door and into the sitting-room, to find his basket and his mistress. But what was this? A big, green-eyed cat glared at him from a basketful of kittens, and then, with one leap, the cat was on Prince, and was scratching him with ten sharp claws!

"Woof, woof!" yelped Prince, and tore back to the kitchen. He heard the canary singing loudly in the window.

"Who's this bad dog, naughty dog? After him, Green-Eyes, after him! Trilla, trilla, trilla!"

Dame Tiptap went into the kitchen. "So you have come back again, Prince!" she said. "I thought you had run away and would never come back. You were so cross and bad-tempered because I had my friends here. I thought you would go to live with someone who was all alone. Surely you do not want to live with me again?"

" Woof, I do, I do, woof ! " said poor Prince, feeling very sad and frightened. " Let me have my lovely basket, and my beautiful dish, Mistress. I will be a good dog now."

" I'm glad to hear that," said Dame Tiptap. " You can certainly live here if you wish, because it is your home. But your basket belongs to Green-Eyes now, and to her darling kittens, and Green-Eyes has your dish to feed from. But, if you like, you can have the kennel in the yard, and the old dish out of the scullery. Keep out of the house, though, Prince, because if you don't I am sure Green-Eyes will fly at you ! "

So poor Prince had to live in the yard and eat from the old scullery dish. He did not dare to go into the house. When he tried to, one cold afternoon, because he badly wanted a warm fire and a nice pat, Green-Eyes flew at him and scratched him all the way down his long nose.

" You keep out ! " hissed Green-Eyes. " This is *my* house, not yours ! You belong to the yard. I don't like dogs. I'll let you live here if you keep to the yard, but not unless ! Mistress has got me and my four kittens, and a singing canary. She can easily do without a vain little dog like you ! "

Prince knew that was true. He lost his pride and his bad temper. He grew used to the kennel in the yard. He gave Dame Tiptap a great welcome whenever she came to see him. He greeted her friends with licks and yelps of joy.

"Quite a different dog!" said everyone. "Perhaps when Green-Eyes' four kittens go to new homes she will make friends with him."

The kittens went to new homes when they were eight weeks old. Green-Eyes no longer felt fierce and protective, anxious to save her kittens from a snapping dog.

Prince spoke to her humbly one day. "It's very cold out

here. Couldn't I come in for a few minutes? I won't lie in your basket."

"All right. But mind—any nonsense and *out you go again !*"

So now Prince sometimes lies by the fire and warms himself, whilst Green-Eyes purrs in the basket nearby. Dame Tiptap knits and smiles to herself. She thinks that Prince will end by being quite a nice, sensible dog after all!

Prince lies there and stares at Green-Eyes—and he thinks to himself: "It seems to me that Green-Eyes is mistress of this house now! Oh for the old days when Dame Tiptap was mistress and I could do what I liked!"

But it was he himself who changed his good luck to bad, wasn't it?

The Little Bully

ONCE upon a time, not so very long ago, there was a small boy called Henry. Although he wasn't very big, he was strong, and he loved to tease all the boys and girls who went to school with him. What he loved most to do was to pinch. How he pinched ! He had strong hands, and he could pinch so hard that he could make a big bruise come in half a second. Another trick he played was pricking people with a pin. He used to keep a pin in his coat, and when a small boy or girl was sitting quietly beside him, reading or working, he would slyly take out his pin and prick them.

So you can guess how all the children hated him. They tried pinching him back, but that was no good because he could always pinch harder than anybody. They didn't like telling their teacher, because that was telling tales.

" He's a nasty little bully," said the boys and girls. " We hope one day he will be properly punished."

Well, that day came, as you will see—but very strangely.

It happened that there was a Sunday-school treat, and the children were to go to the seaside for a whole day. They were most excited. They were to go by train, and to take their lunch with them. They would have tea all together in the tea-rooms by the sea. How they hoped it would be fine !

When the day came, the sun shone out of a deep-blue sky, and all the children were wild with excitement. They crowded into the train and sat down—but nobody wanted to sit next to Henry because he always pinched hard when he was excited. Still, someone had to, because there wasn't room for him to have a carriage all to himself. So Rosie and Margery sat by him, and hoped he would be nice and not bully them.

But, goodness me, how he pinched them! There was no teacher in his carriage, so he pinched Rosie and Margery black and blue, and when the other children shouted at him he took out his pin and vowed he would prick anyone who came near him. Rosie cried and Margery scowled, and, in Henry's carriage, it was a miserable journey down to the sea.

When they arrived at the seaside out jumped all the children with a shout of joy. Down to the sands they raced, hand in hand—but nobody took Henry's hand. Nobody went near him. Nobody played with him. Nobody would help him to dig a castle.

Henry was angry. He went to a sandy corner near a rocky pool and sat down by himself. He took out his lunch and looked at it. It was a good lunch. There were two hard-boiled eggs, six jam sandwiches, three pieces of bread and butter,

a ginger cake, and a bar of chocolate. He would eat it all by himself. He wouldn't offer anyone anything !

Just as he was beginning on the eggs, he heard a hoarse voice near him. " Good morning ! I am *so* pleased to meet a boy like you." Henry turned round and stared in fright. Whatever do you think he saw ?

Henry saw a monster crab walking sideways out of the pool. His eyes were on the ends of short stalks and looked most queer. He held out his front claw to Henry. Henry put out his hand to shake the crab's claw, but to his surprise and anger the crab opened his pincers and nipped his hand so hard that the little boy yelled.

" You horrid thing ! " he wept, nursing his pinched hand. " Pinching me like that ! "

" But surely you are a pincher, like me ? " said the big crab in surprise. " I love pinching, and so do you. Would you like to pinch me back ? "

Henry looked at the crab's hard shell and knew quite well that he could never hurt the crab. Besides, if he tried, it might pinch him again, very hard.

" Ah, here is my good cousin," said the crab pleasantly, and, to Henry's horror, he saw a large sandy lobster crawling heavily out of the pool. Before the little boy could stop him the lobster took his hand in his great pincer-like claws and pinched it so hard that Henry yelled in pain.

" Stop, stop ! You are breaking my hand ! " he cried.

The lobster waved its stalked eyes about and seemed surprised. " But aren't you a pincher like myself ? " he asked in a deep voice. " Come, come, you are making fun of me ! "

He slyly pinched Henry on his fat legs, and the little boy yelled again. Then he stared at the pool in surprise, for out came sandy-coloured shrimps and prawns, more crabs, and another large lobster. The shrimps and prawns had long, needle-like feelers in front of their heads and they pricked

Henry with these, just for fun. The crabs surrounded him so
that he couldn't get away, and, dear me! poor Henry was soon
black and blue with their pinching, and howled every time a
shrimp or prawn pricked him.

"Don't you like it?" said all the creatures in surprise. "Why, we were told you would love to see us because you were a champion pincher and pricker yourself. Come, come— join in the fun!"

Henry leapt to his feet, crying loudly. His lunch rolled into the pool, and when the crabs and lobsters saw it they ran to it and began to feast eagerly. Henry saw that they had forgotten him for a time, and he turned and ran for his life, tears streaming down his cheeks.

He found another corner, far from the water, and sat down to think. He was pinched black and blue and pricked all over. He had lost his lunch, and he had been very much frightened. As he sat thinking, his cheeks became red and he hung his head.

"They only did to me what I keep doing to the other children," he thought. "But how it hurt! And how I hated those crabs and lobsters! I suppose the other children hate me too. Well, I jolly well shan't pinch or prick any more."

And he didn't, though nobody knew why. Henry never told anyone about his seaside adventure, but he had learnt his lesson. I wish all pinchers could learn it, don't you?

D

The Six Little Motor-Cars

HENRY had six little motor-cars, all different. One was a car, one was a lorry, one was a milk-van, one was a bus, one was a racer and the last was a butcher's van.

They were very old, quite four years old. But they all had their wheels, and they all ran well along the nursery floor. It was only their paint that had gone.

The car had once been blue, and the lorry had been brown. The milk-van had been bright yellow, and the bus red. The racer had been green and the butcher's van a brilliant orange. Now all the little cars were grey, without a single bit of their bright colours left.

But Henry still played with them, and loved them. He got them out every week and ran them over the floor, hooting loudly as if he were the six cars. He put them away carefully and didn't tread on them at all.

" How you do love your little cars, Henry ! " said his mother. " They are getting very old. But you must keep them carefully because I haven't any money to buy you nice little cars like that again for a long time ! "

Now one day Thomas and his mother came to tea. He was younger than Henry, and he loved cars even more than Henry did. He had one of his own, quite a big one—but he had no little ones at all. So, when he saw Henry's cars in the toy-cupboard he gave a squeal of delight.

" Oh ! Look at those cars ! Can we play with them ? "

It was nice to have someone else playing at cars, hooting and running them forward and back. The two boys built streets with their bricks and put up posts for traffic lights. It really was great fun.

And then, when Thomas had to go home, he wanted to take the cars with him! His mother shook her head and said no, he couldn't.

"They belong to Henry," she said. "You have played with them all afternoon. Now you must leave them."

Thomas began to scream. Henry looked at him in disgust.

Fancy a boy behaving like that! Why, only babies yelled.

"Oh dear!" said Thomas's mother. "Don't scream, Thomas. You know, Mrs. Hill, he has been very unwell, and I have had to give him his own way a lot. The doctor says it is very bad for him to scream. Now do be sensible, Thomas."

But Thomas was not going to be sensible. He screamed till he was purple in the face.

"Henry," said Henry's mother, "will you lend Thomas your cars just for to-night? You can have them back again to-morrow."

Thomas stopped screaming to hear what Henry would say.

"No," said Henry firmly. "I've never lent my cars to anyone. They are too precious."

"Henry, be unselfish," said his mother. "Do it to please me. Poor Thomas is so unhappy."

Henry looked at his mother.

"Well, Mummy," he said, "I'll lend him them because I want to please you, not because Thomas is unhappy. I think he's naughty, and I don't want him to come to tea again."

Thomas stopped screaming. He looked rather ashamed, but he let his mother put the six cars into his pockets. Henry was sad. He felt sure they would come back broken, with some of the wheels missing. He was sad all that evening. His mother was sorry.

"Henry, I'm glad to have such a kind little boy," she said, when she put him to bed. "You make me very happy."

Well, Henry was glad about that, but he hadn't made himself happy at all ! He thought about his precious cars a great deal, and wondered if Thomas was taking care of them.

Next morning Thomas arrived at the front door, with his father this time, not his mother. In his hand he carried a big box. Henry wondered if all his cars were in it.

Thomas came upstairs with his father and the box. "Now, Thomas, what have you got to say to Henry?" said his father

"Henry, here are your cars," said Thomas, talking as if he were ashamed of himself. "I'm sorry I screamed for them. Daddy was very angry when he knew."

"It's all right," said Henry, taking the box. He didn't like to open it in case he found some of the cars were broken.

"Do open the box," said Thomas. So Henry did open it— and how he stared ! Every single one of those little cars had been given a fresh coat of bright paint! There they were in the box, red, orange, blue, green, brown and yellow! They looked marvellous.

"I did that in return for your kindness," said Thomas's father. "And you will find a nice traffic-light indicator there too. Thomas took money from his money-box and bought it. He's rather ashamed of himself, you see. I'm not surprised you don't want him to come to tea again with you."

"Oh, but I *do*!" cried Henry, quite changing his mind. "I *do*! We had a lovely time yesterday with the cars. Oh, aren't they fine now! As good as new. Better! And look at this lovely traffic light. You can really change the colours."

Thomas came to tea with Henry the next week and the two of them played the whole afternoon with the cars, streets made of bricks and the traffic light. And when it was time for Thomas to go home, did he yell and scream for the cars? Not he!

He went home with his mother, sad to leave the cars, but making up his mind never to behave like a baby again.

Henry's mother watched him putting away the little cars.

"It's a funny thing, Henry," she said, "but whenever anyone does something to please somebody else, it always comes back to them. You pleased *me*—and now Thomas and his father have pleased *you*! I didn't reward you—but they did!"

It's a pity everyone doesn't know that, isn't it? Kindness always comes back somehow.

The Unkind Children

Ping! A stone came flying through the air and almost hit a little sparrow sitting on the fence. It flew away with a chirrup of fright.

"Nearly got that bird," said Robert. "Your turn now, Winnie."

Ping! Winnie's stone hit the wall, and the next-door cat, who was lying asleep there, leapt off with a loud yell.

"Those unkind children again!" she said.

Soon every bird and animal nearby was warned that Winnie and Robert were

throwing
stones
again. Not
a single
one would
go near.
They all
hated the
two un-
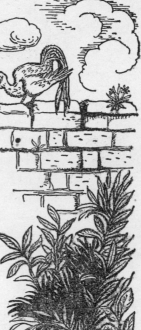
kind children who loved to throw
stones at any living thing.

"Nothing to throw stones at!"
said Winnie. "Let's go for a
walk. Maybe we shall find some
birds down the lane."

Off they went, their hands full
of small stones. They kept a
sharp look-out for any bird in the
hedge or on the telegraph wires.

They came to a low wall that
ran round a garden. Winnie
stopped and pulled Robert's arm.

"Look—what a funny bird!
Do you see it?" Robert looked. He saw a very queer-
looking bird indeed. It was on a level with the wall. It was
red, with yellow wings and a bright green tail.

"See if you can hit it!" said Winnie. Robert took a stone,
and aimed it carefully. It struck the queer bird full on the
back!

"Good shot!" said Winnie.

And then a dreadful thing happened! Somebody stood up
from behind the wall—somebody wearing a hat which was
trimmed with the red and yellow bird! The bird hung sideways from the hat now, looking very queer.

" Oooh ! It was a bird in a hat ! " said Winnie, frightened.

A big woman glared at the two children. She wore a red cloak, the bird-trimmed hat, and big spectacles on her nose.

" Come here ! " she rapped out. " It's time you were taught a lesson ! I'm Mrs. Do-the-Same-to-You ! Maybe you've heard of me ? "

The children hadn't, but they didn't like the sound of her at all. They turned to run away. But in a trice Mrs. Do-the-Same-to-You was over the wall and was holding them firmly by their arms. She had a big bag with her. She opened it and popped the two unkind children into it. It wasn't a bit of good struggling. They couldn't get out.

Mrs. Do-the-Same-to-You took them to her cottage in the middle of the wood. She shook the children out of her bag on to the grass. Bump ! They fell out and yelled.

She took a whistle from her pocket and blew on it. At once a small army of brownies, not much bigger than dolls, came running from the wood.

" These are the Brownie King's pea-shooters," she said to the children. " They don't get enough practice at shooting peas at people. You don't seem to mind hitting others with stones, so I don't expect you'll mind if you are shot at with peas! It will be excellent practice for the pea-shooters."

The children didn't like the sound of this at all. They could see no way of escape, because there was a high wall round the garden, and Mrs. Do-the-Same-to-You stood by the only gate. They tried to run behind a bush.

The brownie pea-shooters all had little blow-pipes and bags of hard, dried peas. Quick as lightning, they slipped peas into their mouths and blew them hard out of the blow-pipes or pea-shooters.

Ping! The first one hit Winnie on the nose.

Ping! Another one hit Robert on the ear.

Ping! Ping! Ping! Three peas hit the children hard on hand, knee and neck. They yelled.

"This is good sport!" cried the little brownies. "Are

you sure it's all right for us to practise on these children, Mrs. Do-the-Same-to-You?"

"Oh, quite," she said. "I found them throwing stones at birds. They can't object to you shooting peas at them! After all, you are doing much the same thing, but using peas instead of stones."

"Stop! Stop!" cried the children. "The peas hurt. They sting! Oh, stop!"

"Well, don't stones hurt, too?" asked Mrs.

Do-the-Same-to-You. "Perhaps you would rather the pea-shooters shot stones?"

"Oh no, oh no!" cried Winnie. "Stones would be worse. Oh, let us go! That pea nearly went into my eye."

Ping! Ping! Ping! Ping! The little pea-shooters were having a fine time. The children dodged here and there, they tried to hide behind trees and bushes, they ran to corners, but always the brownies followed them, blowing hard peas at them and hardly ever missing. Soon the children were covered with red spots where the peas had hit them, and they began to feel very sorry for themselves indeed.

Mrs. Do-the-Same-to-You went indoors to put her kettle on to boil. As soon as Robert saw that she had left the gate, he took Winnie's hand and dragged her there. In a trice he had it open and the two children shot through it.

After them poured the delighted brownies, shooting peas as hard as they could! They chased Winnie and Robert all

the way to the edge of the wood. Ping, ping, ping, ping, went the peas. You should have heard the children yell!

They got home at last, tears running down their faces. They rubbed the red places that the peas had hit.

" Horrid little brownies ! " sobbed Winnie.

" Unkind little creatures ! " wept Robert.

" How dare they, how dare they ? " cried Winnie. " Just look at all the places on my face, hands and knees ! I'm hurting all over ! "

" Wait till I see that nasty Mrs. Do-the-Same-to-You ! " yelled Robert. " I'll tell her what I think of her ! I'll throw a big stone at her ! "

But when he met her, he didn't say a word and he didn't throw a stone. In fact, neither he nor Winnie have ever thrown a stone at anything again. They know now how it hurts to have something hitting you hard. They still have little red spots where those peas struck them.

I don't feel a bit sorry for them, do you ?

The Little Paper-Folk

ONE very wet afternoon Jimmy and Susan thought they would borrow two pairs of Nurse's scissors and cut out pictures from a book. Nurse said they might, so they found the scissors, took two old books from the newspaper-rack in the dining-room, and went to the nursery to cut out.

"I'm going to cut out these motor-cars," said Jimmy. "They're fine ones, all in colour. Look, Susan."

"Yes," said Susan. "Well, I shall cut out some people. See, there's an old woman carrying a basket, and a tall man in a pointed hat, and a little man in a dressing-gown. I shall cut out lots of people."

Jimmy soon cut out his motor-cars. There were three—one red, one green, and one blue. Then he thought he would cut out smaller things. There was a poker, a pair of tongs, and a coal-shovel on one page, so he cut those out. Then he found a page of boxes of chocolates, all with their lids open to show the chocolates inside. They did look delicious.

"I shall cut out these boxes of chocolates," he said to Susan. "Oh, what a nice lot of little people you have cut out! Stand them up against something, Susan. They will look real then."

Susan stood them up. There was the old woman, the tall man, the little man in a dressing-gown, a black imp, and a fat boy bowling a hoop. She stood them all up against a book.

"We've cut out lots of things," she said, "cars and people, fire-irons, and boxes of chocolates. Oh, Jimmy, wouldn't it be lovely if those chocolates were real?"

"Let's take everything we've cut out to the big window-sill," said Jimmy, gathering up his paper cars and other things.

"We'll stand the cars up and the people too. They will look fine."

So they went to the window-sill, behind the big blue curtain, and began to stand up all their paper things.

"I wish, I wish we were as small as these little people," said Susan. "Then we could play with them and see what they are really like."

Well, I don't quite know how it happened, but there must have been some magic about that day, for no sooner had Susan wished her wish than it came true!

Yes, it really did! She and Jimmy grew smaller and smaller and they felt very much out of breath, for it all happened so quickly. But when at last they stopped growing small, they found themselves on the window-sill with the paper people and cars. And the paper people were alive!

They smiled at Susan and Jimmy, and came to shake hands with them. Their hands were funny—all flat and papery—and when the old woman turned round Jimmy saw that she hadn't a proper back—there were printed letters all over her!

"That's the other side of the page she was cut out of!" whispered Jimmy, as he saw Susan's look of surprise. "There was a story the other side, and that's part of it. Isn't it queer?"

"We are glad you cut out such lovely boxes of chocolates for us," said the man in the pointed hat, picking up a box and looking at it.

"And I'm glad you cut out my hoop for me," said the little fat boy. He raised his stick to trundle his hoop, but, alas, it would not roll properly, because Susan's scissors had cut right through the hoop in one little place.

The boy was cross. "The hoop won't roll properly," he said frowning. "You were careless when you cut it out! I don't like you after all!"

"Don't take any notice of him," said the little man in the dressing-gown. "He's a bad-natured boy. I am pleased with the way you cut out my dressing-gown. Look, even my girdle is well cut out, so that I can tie it round me."

The man in the pointed hat picked up a box of chocolates and offered them to Susan.

But she couldn't get her fingers into the box! You see, it was only a painted box, so of course the chocolates couldn't be taken out. She was so disappointed.

" I can't take out any of the chocolates," she said, trying hard.

The black imp she had cut out came and looked at the box. He put up his little black hand, and, to Susan's surprise, he picked out a handful of the chocolates and ran off with them.

" I expect he can do it because he's made of paper like the chocolates," whispered Jimmy. " Anyway, they'd taste horrid, I'm sure ! "

" Let's go for a ride in these cars," cried the old woman with the basket. They ran to the cars. The tall man took the wheel of the red car and the old lady climbed in beside him. That left the imp all alone with the green car, and he looked as black as thunder.

" I can't drive a car," he said. " One of you children must get in with me and drive me along. I'm not going to be left out ! "

" I don't want to get in that car with you," said Jimmy. " You look so black and dirty."

" You nasty boy ! " cried the imp, in a rage. " Get into the car at once. How dare you insult one of the paper-folk ! "

To Jimmy's surprise all the other paper-folk sided with the black imp. They shouted angrily to the children :

" Get in and drive him ! Get in and drive him ! You wouldn't eat our chocolates, and now you are too grand to drive our car ! "

The children felt quite scared. Jimmy went to the green car and tried to get in. But of course he couldn't, because it was only paper. He tried and tried, but his leg simply slid down the paper to the ground.

The imp was sitting at the back, watching. He frowned at Jimmy, and cried out crossly :

" You're only pretending not to be able to get in. You're only pretending ! Why can't you get in ? You're the same as us, aren't you, and *we* got in ! "

" Well, we're *not* the same as you, so there ! " said Jimmy, losing his temper. " You're only made of paper—you haven't even got proper backs ! We're real. You're just cut-out people ; and your cars are cut-out cars, so of course we can't get into them ! Don't be so silly ! "

Well, when the paper-folk heard Jimmy saying that, they were all as hurt and angry as could be. They climbed out of the cars and looked all round them for something to fight the children with. They suddenly saw the poker, the tongs, and the shovel that Jimmy had cut out, lying on the ground by the boxes of chocolates.

The tall man picked up the poker, and the man in the dressing-gown picked up the tongs. The imp snatched up the shovel. The old woman took her basket, and the boy took his hoop-stick to fight with, and together all the paper-folk rushed angrily at the scared children.

" Don't be frightened, Susan," said Jimmy. " They're only paper."

" But we haven't anything to fight them with," cried Susan, looking round on the window-sill.

" Let's blow them with our breath," shouted Jimmy. " They are only paper, you know."

So, much to the cut-out people's surprise, as soon as they were close to the children Jimmy and Susan blew hard at them with all their breath.

" Wheeeeeeeeeeeeeeew ! " went the children together, and the paper-folk were all blown over flat ! What a surprise for

them! They picked themselves up again and rushed at the
children once more.

"Wheeeeeeeeeeeeeeew!" blew Jimmy and Susan, and once
again the paper-folk were blown down flat—and, oh my,
the fat boy was blown right over the edge of the window-sill
on to the floor below. How the paper-folk screamed to see
him go!

"I shan't have much breath left soon," whispered Jimmy
to Susan. "Whatever shall we do?"

"I wish we could grow to our own size again," wailed
Susan, who had had quite enough of being small.

Well, she had only to wish that for it to become true, for there was still a little magic floating about in the air. Just as the paper-folk were rushing at them again the children shot up tall, and the cut-out people cried out in surprise.

In a trice the children were their own size, and at that moment they heard Nurse's voice.

"Wherever are you? Jimmy! Susan! I've been looking for you everywhere!"

"Here we are, Nurse," said Jimmy, peeping round the window-curtain.

"But you weren't there a minute ago, Jimmy, for I looked to see," said Nurse in astonishment. "There were only a few bits of paper blowing about on the window-sill. Now, where have you been hiding?"

"Truly we were there, Nurse," said Jimmy, and he and Susan told her of their adventure with the paper-folk.

But Nurse laughed and wouldn't believe it. "Don't make up such silly tales," she said. "Fighting with paper-folk indeed! Whoever heard such nonsense?"

"Well, Nurse, look!" cried Susan, suddenly. "Here's that nasty little fat boy on the floor, with his hoop. Jimmy blew him over the edge of the window-sill. That just proves we are telling the truth."

It did, didn't it? The children and Nurse looked at the paper-boy on the floor, and at the other paper-folk who were all lying quietly on the window-sill.

"I should paste them fast into your scrap-book," said Nurse. "Then they won't do any more mischief!"

So that's where the paper-folk are now—in the middle of the scrap-book, pasted down tightly. You can see them there any time you go to tea with Jimmy and Susan!

The Tiresome Poker

ONCE when Sleeky the pixie went by Dame Ricky's cottage, he heard her talking to Mother Goody over the fence.

"My dear!" said Dame Ricky. "I *was* in a way this morning, I can tell you! When I went to light the kitchen fire, I found I hadn't a bit of firewood in the house. It was my baking day, too."

"You should have borrowed some firewood from me!" said Mother Goody.

"Well, I would, my dear," said Dame Ricky, "but I suddenly remembered that old magic poker that belonged to my grandmother—you know, the poker with the red knob at the top. I always used to use it to light my fires—and then it got rather tiresome and talkative and I put it away."

"Dear me! I haven't heard of the magic poker before," said Mother Goody. "Tell me about it. How does it light a fire?"

"Oh, you just stick it into the empty fireplace and put a few coals on top," said Dame Ricky. "Then you say, 'Poker, light up!' and in half a minute there's a wonderful fire burning away!"

"Well, well," said Mother Goody, surprised. "That's a useful poker to be sure!"

Now Sleeky the pixie heard all this and he couldn't help feeling a bit excited. And that afternoon, when Dame Ricky had gone shopping, Sleeky slipped along to her house and looked into her kitchen.

There, standing by the fireplace was a big poker with a red

knob at the end. " That's the one ! " said Sleeky, pleased.
" I'll borrow you for a few days—but I shan't tell Dame
Ricky ! "

He ran off with the poker. He thought he would try to light
his fire with it, because it had gone out twice that day. He
put the poker into his fireplace and piled coals on top.

" Poker, light up ! " said Sleeky. And the poker made a
sizzling noise as if it were getting hot, and then the coals
burst into flame. A beautiful fire burnt in the fireplace, as hot
as could be !

" How marvellous ! " said Sleeky, very pleased. He took
the poker out, and stood it by the fireplace. It sizzled for a
little while and then made no more noise.

Soon Hallo the brownie came in to see Sleeky. He looked
at the roaring fire.

" Fine fire, that ! " said Hallo, rubbing his hands together.

" Yes, I'm good at getting a hot fire going," said Sleeky.

" So am I," said a sharp voice from somewhere. " But I

don't know what Dame Ricky will say when she knows what
you've done."

Sleeky looked all round in alarm. Hallo looked most
astonished. "What have you been doing to make Dame
Ricky cross?" he asked.

"Nothing at all," said Sleeky.

"Fibber! Story-teller!" said the voice again, and the
poker jiggled itself a little.

"It's the poker talk-
ing!" cried Hallo, and
he shot out of the house
at once. Sleeky glared at
the poker in a rage.

"How dare you inter-
fere when I am talking to
my friends?"
he cried.

"I shall say
what I like,
when I like,
and how I
like," said the
poker, banging itself against the wall. "I'm a very old and
wise poker."

"You're not. You're silly and stupid and interfering,"
said Sleeky. "If you're not careful I'll take you back to
Dame Ricky and tell her you came here all by yourself."

"Naughty little story-teller!" said the poker in a shocked
voice. "Yes—you must take me back to Dame Ricky, and
see what *I'll* tell her! My goodness me—what a lovely
spanking you will get!"

Sleeky stared at the poker in alarm and anger. What could
you do with a poker like that? No wonder Dame Ricky
said it was a tiresome poker, and put it away!

There was
a knock at
the door. In
came Snibble
the goblin.
"Hallo,
Sleeky," said
Snibble.
"Could you
possibly
spare me a
box of
matches? I'd
like some to
light my fire, and I haven't any."

"Neither have I," said Sleeky. And then he had a fine idea. "But I've got a magic poker here—take it and use that, if you like."

The poker did a real dance of rage in the fireplace. "Lending me here, there, and everywhere!" it cried. "Who do you think I am? Look on the stove over there, Snibble, and you'll find matches all right. Sleeky is a mean old story-teller, and a naughty little thief, too!"

"Is that—is that—can it be—the *poker* talking?" said Snibble, scared as could be.

Sleeky nodded. "It's a dreadful poker," he said gloomily. "It just interferes in everything. Talks all the time, and says the most dreadful things. Do take it, Snibble, please do."

"No, thank you," said Snibble, and he went away in such a hurry that he forgot all about the matches. The poker laughed loudly and jiggled itself in a most annoying manner.

"Stop fidgeting," ordered Sleeky.

The poker jiggled all the more, and even began to whistle. Sleeky got angrier and angrier. He suddenly got up, ran over to the poker, took it into his hand and threw it right out of the window!

Oh, goodness gracious! It hit Mister Slow-Foot on the shoulder, and he looked round in surprise and anger.

"Who did that? Who did that?" he shouted. Sleeky hid behind the window curtains. He was afraid of Mister Slow-Foot. The poker stood up on its one leg and spoke politely to Slow-Foot.

"It was Sleeky who threw me at you. He's a bad pixie."

Mr. Slow-Foot went to Sleeky's house and in half a minute you might have heard a sound of smacking and crying, for although Slow-Foot was slow of foot he was mighty quick of hand!

Sleeky sat crying in a chair by the fire. He wiped his eyes and said to himself: "Well, anyway, that horrible poker is gone. I hope it won't tell tales of me to Dame Ricky."

There was a knock at the door. Tap-tap-tap! Tap-tap-tap!

"Come in!" shouted Sleeky, wiping the last tears away. But nobody came in. "COME IN!" yelled Sleeky, getting cross.

Tap-tap-tap ! Tap-tap-tap ! Sleeky got annoyed and went to the door. He opened it—and oh dear, in hopped that poker on its one steel leg, as lively as could be !

" Thanks ! " said the poker. " Couldn't reach the handle myself. Well—I'm back, you see. You don't look very pleased to see me ! "

It went back to its place by the fire. Sleeky glared at it. " Pleased to see you ! " he cried. " I should just think I'm not ! Go out ! I will NOT have you in my house."

" I'm sorry about that," said the poker, leaning back against the wall. " I mean to stay, you see."

Well, that poker meant what it said. No matter how Sleeky begged it, scolded it, even cried tears to it, it just said the same thing.

" I mean to stay ! "

And oh, what a nuisance it was all that day ! How it chattered and talked ! What dreadful things it said !

" Sleeky, you'd better get rid of that poker," said Feefo, when he came in for a few minutes. " No one will come and see you if you let it stand there and say cheeky things."

When Sleeky was alone after tea he sat and stared at the poker. How could he get rid of it? Ah—he would put it into the dust-bin—and then the dustman would take it away to-morrow. That would be fine!

He waited until the poker seemed to be asleep. Then he quickly took hold of it, rushed out into the yard and threw it into the dust-bin! Clang! The lid went on—the poker was a prisoner among the tea-leaves and the cinders!

"That's finished *you*!" said Sleeky, fiercely, as he heard the poker begin to jiggle against the lid. "You can't get out of there! You won't annoy me any more with your tiresome ways!"

But Sleeky was wrong. Just wait and see what that tiresome poker did!

That evening Higgle the brownie came in to have supper with Sleeky. Sleeky liked Higgle. He was a generous fellow, and always brought a present of some kind with him. This evening he brought four sausage rolls, which smelt most delicious.

The two of them sat down to eat the sausage rolls, with pickles, bread and coffee. Just as they were in the middle of the meal there came a tapping at the window.

Tap-tap-tap ! Tap-tap-tap !

Well, of course, Sleeky knew quite well what was making that noise—the poker ! He had just heard a crash—that was the dust-bin lid falling on the ground—and now came the tap-tap-tap. Bother that poker ! It wanted to come indoors again. Well, Sleeky was quite determined to take no notice of it.

Tap-tap-tap ! Tap-tap-tap !

" Sleeky, what's that noise ? " asked Higgle.

" Tree against the window, I expect," said Sleeky. " Take no notice."

Tap-tap-tap ! Tap-tap-tap !

" Funny sort of tree," said Higgle, puzzled.

" Let me in ! " suddenly yelled the poker.

" That tree wants to come in ! " said Higgle, in astonishment.

" Take no notice," said Sleeky, in a rage. But it wasn't a bit of good taking no notice—because the poker suddenly tapped so hard that it broke the window.

CRASH ! Down came the glass in tiny bits, and Higgle and Sleeky almost jumped out of their skins ! The poker hopped in and went to the fire. It was shivering.

" Mean creature ! " it said to Sleeky. " Putting me in the dust-bin with tea-leaves and things ! I'm cold. I'm going to stand here and tell you exactly what I think of you. You're a nasty, mean fellow, and I don't like you a bit. You're a horrid. . . ."

Higgle stared in horror at the magic poker, feeling quite frightened. Sleeky was so angry that he nearly burst with rage. He jumped up and ran to the poker. He picked it up and shouted :

" Ho, so you think you'll stand there and be rude to

me, do you? Well, you won't! I'll put you into the village
pond! It's deep—and cold—and wet! Ho, ho—you'll be
sorry you ever came back to me when you go splash into the
pond!"

And out he went into the night with the poker. Higgle
sat and stared—and then he felt a bit frightened and got up
to put on his coat. He went home, wondering how in the
world Sleeky had got hold of such a peculiar poker.

Sleeky went to the village pond. The poker wriggled about
in his hand for all it was worth, trying to get away, but it
couldn't. And into the pond it went, flying high into the air,
and then down, down, down into the cold water, splash!
It disappeared. It was gone.

"Good!" said Sleeky. "That's the end of you!"

The pixie went home. He finished up the sausage rolls
and pickles, and then he went to bed. He got himself a
hot-water bottle, because he was cold. He was soon fast
asleep.

In the middle of the night he woke up very suddenly. What could that noise be? He could hear funny footsteps coming down the lane. Tip-tap, tip-tap, tip-tap! Sleeky sat up in bed and listened.

"Oh my, oh my, I hope it isn't that horrid, nasty poker!" he groaned. "Oh, I really couldn't bear it. Oh, what ever shall I do?"

Tip-tap, tip-tap! The noise came nearer and nearer. It came to Sleeky's gate. It stopped there. The gate creaked as it opened.

Tip-tap, tip-tap! The noise came up the garden-path. Then there came a rapping on the door below.

"Well, knock all you like, I'll not let you in!" said Sleeky fiercely. "Wake everyone up if you like—but I'll NOT LET YOU IN!"

The poker stopped knocking after a while. It went to the broken window. It got in through there, and Sleeky heard it land with a bump on the floor.

"Well, maybe the horrid thing will put itself by the fire and stay quiet," thought the pixie, lying down again.

But after a bit Sleeky heard the poker grumbling away to itself downstairs.

"The fire's out! It's cold as ice in this kitchen. I'm wet and shivering! Oooooooooosh! I shall catch such a cold. A-tish-oo!"

Then there came the noise of the poker coming upstairs. Tip-tap, tip-tap, tip-tap! Quick as lightning Sleeky jumped out of bed and shut his door. Then back to bed he went again, grinning to himself. The poker got to the door. It knocked on it.

Tap-tap-tap! Sleeky pretended to snore. The poker knocked again, more loudly. TAP-TAP-TAP!

Sleeky snored again. The poker shouted angrily. "You're not asleep. I know you're not. I heard you get out of bed

just now. If you don't open the door to me I'll go downstairs and break all your cups and saucers, dishes and glasses. Yes, I will, I will!"

"You wicked poker!" cried Sleeky, in a rage, quite forgetting to be asleep.

"I'm going downstairs to break the cups to begin with," said the poker and tip-tapped down a few steps. But Sleeky leapt out of bed at once and opened the door.

"Don't you dare to do a thing like that!" he shouted. "Just don't you dare!"

The poker hopped up the stairs again and into the bedroom. Sleeky sulkily got into bed. The poker hopped over to the bed and tried to get in between the sheets.

"Look here! What are you doing?" cried Sleeky. "Get out of my bed, you nasty, wet, cold thing!"

"Well, who made me cold and wet?" said the poker, getting right into bed. "You did! Now you can just warm me up. Let me cuddle close to you. Oooooh—that's better."

"You're sticking into me," said Sleeky, pushing the poker away. "You're hurting me. You're all wet. Get away."

But Sleeky might as well have talked to the moon for all the notice that poker took! It just stuck itself well into Sleeky and warmed itself on him. After a bit the pixie simply couldn't bear it. He got out of bed, found a rug, and went to sleep on the floor.

Then the poker was happy. It had a warm bed all to itself, and a hot-water bottle. My, it was lovely!

In the morning Sleeky was very miserable. He was stiff and cold with sleeping on the floor. The poker popped its knobbly head up and spoke to him.

"I like living with you. You've got a nice warm fire in your kitchen, and a nice warm bed at night. Go down and light the fire before I get up. Then the kitchen will be warm."

Sleeky didn't say a word. He just felt that he couldn't do anything with a poker like that. He dressed himself and then slipped out of the house. He went to Dame Ricky's and knocked on her door.

She opened it in surprise. "What do you want so early in the morning, Sleeky?" she asked.

"Please, Dame Ricky, I took your poker the other day," said Sleeky, hanging his head.

"Oh, so it was you, was it?" said Dame Ricky. "I wondered who it was. Well, though it was a very naughty thing to do, I'm very, very glad you took it. I always wanted to get rid of that cheeky, talkative poker."

"Dame Ricky, please come and take it back," said Sleeky. "I can't tell you how awful it has been to me. I simply can't tell you! It has broken my kitchen window. And last night it got into bed with me, all wet and cold—and I had to sleep on the floor."

Dame Ricky began to laugh. "Sleeky, I can't help thinking you've been well punished," she said. "You're a naughty little pixie, you know—a very naughty little pixie. And now,

for once in a way you've met something that has got the better of you."

"Dame Ricky, don't laugh," said Sleeky, beginning to cry bitterly. "Please, please come and take the poker away. I'm very unhappy about it."

"A little unhappiness will do you a lot of good," said Dame Ricky. "No—I tell you I don't want the poker back. I'm glad to be rid of it. Now, you go back and get your breakfast. Take no notice of the poker, and maybe it will get tired of talking."

Poor Sleeky! He went back home very sad. The poker was still in bed. It yelled out to Sleeky to light the kitchen fire at once. But Sleeky didn't. He got himself a quick breakfast and then he went to Higgle's.

"Higgle, you said the other day that if I wanted some work to do you'd give me a job in your shop," he said. "Well, I do want some work to do—work that will take

E

me out of my house all day long.   So will you give me that
job ? "

" Certainly," said Higgle.   " It will be very good for you
to have a job.   Start to-day if you like ! "

So Sleeky started his job that very day—and the poker
didn't have a kitchen fire to warm itself by after all.   What a
time it gave poor Sleeky when he got home that night !

" You won't get a fire at all," said Sleeky fiercely.   " I'm
going to be at work all day long, so there !   You'd better go
and find somebody else to annoy, you nasty, horrid thing ! "

Well, well—it's done Sleeky good to have work to do.   As
for that poker, it's making up its mind to move somewhere
where there's a good fire every day.   Tell me if it comes to
you, won't you !

The Enchanted Table

ONCE upon a time there was a strange table. It was perfectly round, and had four strong legs ending in feet like a lion's—paws with claws. Round its edge there was carved a circle of tiny animals—mice, cats, dogs, weasels, rats, pigs, and others.

For many years this table stood in the kitchen of a tailor named Snip, and no one knew of its magic powers. Mrs. Snip laid a white cloth on it each meal time and spread it with food and drink. Once a week she polished it. All the little Snip children sat round it three times a day and, dear me, how they kicked it with their fidgety feet! How they stained it when they spilt their tea! How they marked it with their knives, pens and pencils!

One day an old man came to see Snip the tailor. Mrs. Snip asked him into the kitchen for a cup of tea, and he suddenly saw the table, with its edge of carved animals and its four paws for feet. His eyes opened wide, and he gasped for breath.

" That table ! " he cried. " It's magic ! Didn't you know ? "

" How is it magic ? " asked Mrs. Snip, not believing him at all.

" Look ! " cried the old man. He went up to the table and ran his fingers round the carved animals. He pressed first a mouse, then a cat, then a pig, then a weasel, muttering a few strange words as he did so. Then he tapped each of the four paw-like feet with his right hand.

" Mercy on us ! " cried Mrs. Snip, in horror and surprise. " Look at that ! Why, it's alive ! "

" Wait ! " said the old man, in excitement. " Let me show what it can do now ! "

He went to the table and put his hands on the middle of it. Then, knocking three times sharply, he said: "Bacon and sausages! New bread! Hot cocoa!"

And, would you believe it, a dish of bacon and sausages, a loaf of new bread, and a jug of hot cocoa suddenly appeared on that strange table!

Mrs. Snip couldn't believe her eyes! She sat down on a chair and opened and shut her mouth like a fish, trying to

say something. At last she called the tailor in from the shop.

When she told him what had happened he was amazed.

The old man knocked three times on the table again and said: "Two pineapples! Stewed mushrooms!"

Immediately two large pineapples arrived, and a heap of stewed mushrooms planted themselves in the middle of the dish of bacon and sausages. They smelt very nice.

"Can we eat these things?" asked Mr. Snip at last.

"Of course," said the old man. They all sat down and began to eat. My, how delicious everything was! The table kept quite still, except that once it held out a paw to the fire, and frightened the tailor so much that he swallowed a whole sausage at once and nearly choked.

"This table is worth a lot of money," said the old man. "You should sell it, Snip. It's hundreds of years old, and was made by the gnome Brinnen, in a cave in the heart of a mountain. How did you come to have it ? "

" Oh, it belonged to my father, and to his father, and to *his* father ; in fact, it has been in our family for ages," said the tailor. " But I didn't know it was magic."

" I expect someone forgot how to set the spell working," said the old man. " Look, I'll show you what I did. First you press *this* animal—then you press *this* one—and then *this* —and *this*—and all the time you say some magic words, which I will whisper into your ear for fear someone hears them."

He whispered. The tailor listened in delight.

" And then," said the old man, " just put your hands in the middle of the table—so—and think what food you want. Then rap smartly three times on the top of the table and call out for what you'd like ! "

" Marvellous ! " said the tailor, rubbing his hands together. " Wonderful ! But I shan't sell my table, friend. No, it has been in my family so long that I could not part with it. I will keep it and let it provide food for me and my family."

" Well, treat it kindly," said the old man, putting on his hat to go. " It has feelings, you know. Treat it kindly. It likes a good home. And don't forget to say those magic words once a week."

" Come and dine with us each Sunday," said the tailor. " If it hadn't been for you we should never have found out the magic."

Well, at first all the tailor's children and friends couldn't say enough about that marvellous table. They simply delighted in rapping on it and ordering meals. It didn't matter what they asked for it came. Even when Amelia Snip, the eldest child, rapped and asked for ice-cream pickles they appeared on the table in an instant.

What parties the Snips gave ! Roasted chickens, legs of pork, suet puddings, mince pies, apple tarts, sugar biscuits, six different sorts of cheese—everything was there and nobody ever went short.

The table seemed quite content, except that it would keep walking over to the fire, and sometimes it stroked someone's leg, and made that guest jump nearly out of his skin.

But one day the table became impatient. Six little Snip children sat round it, and they were very fidgety. Amelia kicked one table-leg. Albert kicked another. Harriet spilt her lemonade over it and made it sticky. Paul cut a tiny hole in it with his new penknife. Susan scratched it with her finger-nails. And Bobbo swung his legs up high and kicked the underneath of the table very hard indeed.

The table suddenly lost its temper. It lifted up a paw and smacked Bobbo hard on his bare leg.

"Ooh!" cried Bobbo, slipping down from his chair in a hurry. "Horrid table! It slapped me!"

"How dare you slap my brother!" cried Amelia, and kicked the table-leg hard. It immediately lifted up its paw, put out its claws, and scratched her like a cat!

"Ow!" cried Amelia, and she ran to the shop, howling. Soon the tailor and his wife came back with her, and the tailor scolded the table.

But instead of listening humbly, the table put up a big paw and slapped Mr. Snip! Then it got up and walked over to the fire.

"How many times have I told you that you are *not* to stand so close to the fire?" scolded Mrs. Snip. "No one can sit at you if you do that. It's too hot."

The table ran up to Mrs. Snip and with two of its great paws it pushed her into a chair. Then it shook one of its paws at her crossly and went back to the fire again. Mrs. Snip was very angry.

"Ho!" she said. "So that's how you're feeling, is it? Well, I'll give you some work to do."

She went over to it and rapped smartly on the top three times, calling out: "Roast beef! Roast pork! Roast mutton! Steak-and-kidney pie! Suet roll! Jam sandwich! Currant cake! Plum pudding!" and so on and so on, everything she could think of! The table soon groaned under the weight of all the food she called for, and its four legs almost bent under their burden.

"There!" said the tailor's wife. "That will punish you for your spitefulness!"

But the table had had enough of the Snip family. It had never liked them, for they were mean and selfish. So it made up its mind to go away from the house and never to come back.

It walked slowly to the door, groaning again under the weight of all its dishes. Mrs. Snip and the tailor guessed what it was trying to do, and they rushed at it to push it back. The table rose up on two of its legs and began to punch with its other two.

Crash! Smash! Bang! Splosh! Every dish on the table slid off to the floor! There lay meat, pudding, pie, cakes, everything, and a whole heap of broken china. My, what a mess!

The table was pleased to be rid of its burden. It capered about and gave Mr. Snip a punch on the nose. The tailor was frightened and angry. He really didn't know how to fight a fierce table like this. He tried to get hold of the two legs, but suddenly great claws shot out of the table's paws and scratched him on the hand.

Then the table slapped Mrs. Snip and smacked Amelia and Paul hard. Then it squeezed itself out of the door and ran away down the street. It went on all-fours as soon as it left the house, and was so pleased with itself that it capered about in a very extraordinary way, making everyone run to their windows and doors in amazement.

Well, of course, the news soon went round that the marvellous magic table was loose in the land. Everyone secretly hoped to get it, and everyone was on the look-out for it. But the table was artful. It hid when the evening came and thought hard what it wanted to do.

" I will put myself into a museum," said the table to itself. " A museum is a place where all sorts of interesting and marvellous things are kept for people to wonder at and admire. I will find a museum and go there. Perhaps no one will notice that I have come, and I shall have peace for a while."

It wandered out into the street again, and went to the next town. It was a big one, and the table felt sure it would have a museum. So it had—but the door was shut.

The table looked round the building to see if a window was open. Sure enough there was one, but rather high up. However, the table cared nothing for that. It climbed up a rain-pipe with all its four paws, and squeezed itself in at the window. Then it clambered down the wall inside and looked about for somewhere to stand.

Not far away was a big four-poster bed, a square table, and two solid-looking chairs. They had all belonged to some famous man. The table thought it might as well go and stand with these things, so off it went, and arranged itself in front of the chairs. Then it went comfortably to sleep.

But in the morning it was, of course, discovered at once ! The museum-keeper saw it first, and perhaps he would not have known it was the lost magic table if the table had not suddenly scratched one of its legs with a paw, nearly making the poor man faint with amazement.

" It's the enchanted table ! " he cried, and ran off to spread the news.

Soon the room was quite full of people, all staring and exclaiming, wondering how in the world the table had got into their museum. Then of course began the rapping and the commanding of all kinds of food to appear. The table sighed. It was getting very tired of bearing the weight of so many heavy dishes. It was surprised to think that people seemed so often hungry.

It didn't like being in the museum after all. It was dreadfully cold ; there was no fire there, as there had been at the tailor's, and a terrible draught blew along the floor. The table shivered so much that all the dishes on it shook and shivered too.

That afternoon a message arrived from the King himself. He wanted the marvellous table in his palace. It would save him such a lot of money in feasts, he thought, and it would bring him quite a lot of fame.

The table heard the people talking to the messenger, and it felt quite pleased. It would be warmer in the palace, at any rate. It got up and walked to the door. The people ran away as it came near, for they had heard how it had fought the tailor's family and defeated them.

But the table didn't want to fight. It just wanted to get somewhere nice and warm. The museum-keeper tried to shut the door to stop it from going out, but the table pushed him over, and went out, doing a jig to keep itself warm. It meant to walk to the palace.

Everyone thought that it was going to run away again, and men, women, and children followed it to see what it was going to do. They were filled with surprise to see it mounting the palace steps one by one, and entering the palace doors!

" It's gone to see the King ! " they cried.

The table walked into the palace, and no one tried to stop it, for all the footmen and soldiers were too surprised to move. The table went into the King's study, and found the King there, writing a letter.

" Who is it. Who is it? " asked His Majesty crossly, not looking up. " How many times have I said that people must knock before they interrupt me ? "

The table went up to the King and bowed so low that it knocked its carved edge on the floor. Then it stood up and saluted with one of its paws.

The King looked up—and in a trice he sprang from his chair and ran to the other side of the room in fright, for he had never seen a table like that before.

The table went over to the fire to warm itself. Soon the King recovered from his fright and called his servants.

"Here is that wonderful table," he said. "Take it into my dining-hall, and send out invitations to all the kings, queens, princes, and princesses living near to come and feast to-night. Tell them they shall each have what they like to eat and drink."

The table went into the gold-and-silver dining-hall, and thought it was very grand indeed, but cold. It pointed one of its paws at the empty grate, but as nobody imagined that a table could feel cold, no notice was taken at all. So the table contented itself with doing a little dance to warm itself whenever it began to shiver, and this amused all the servants very much.

When the time for the feast drew near, the footmen laid a wonderful golden cloth on the table-top. Then they set out golden plates and dishes, golden spoons and forks, and golden-handled knives. How they glittered and shone!

No food was put there, not even bread. No, the table was to supply that.

Soon all the guests arrived, and how they stared to see such an empty table! "Nothing but a vase of flowers!" whispered King Piff to Queen Puff.

"Take your seats," said the King, smiling. "I have brought you here to-night to see my new magic table, as enchanted and as bewitched as any table can be! Behold!"

He rapped three times smartly on the table. "A dish of crusty rolls! Some slices of new-made toast!" he cried.

Before his guests' wondering eyes these things appeared, and the King bowed a little as if he were a conjurer performing tricks.

"Now, Queen Puff," he said, "kindly say what you would like for your dinner, and I will see that it comes. Rap three times on the table before saying."

Queen Puff did as she was told. "Celery soup, stewed shark's fin, roast chicken, roast beef, cauliflower, potatoes, and plum pudding!" she said, all in one breath. "Oh, and ginger-beer to drink!"

One by one all the guests wished for the dinner they wanted and marvelled to see everything appear on the table in a trice, all steaming hot and beautifully cooked. They sat and ate, lost in wonder. Then King Piff had an idea.

"I say," he said to the King who had invited him, "won't it give you—er—gold, for instance?"

Everybody there listened breathlessly, for one and all they loved gold, and wanted as much as they could get.

"Well," said the King, "I've never tried anything but food. Perhaps it would spoil the magic of the table if we did. We'd better not."

"Pooh! You mean to try when we're not here, so that you can get as much gold as you want for yourself!"

"Yes, you old miser!" cried Prince Bong, and everyone began to talk at once. The King was horrified to hear himself called such names, and he threatened to call in his soldiers and have everyone arrested.

No one listened to him. They were all rapping hard on the poor table, crying out such things as: "A bag of gold! A sack of gold! Twenty diamonds! Six rubies! A box of jewels! Twenty sacks of gold! A hundred bars of gold!"

The poor table began to tremble. It had never been asked for such things before, and had always been able to give what was demanded. But the magic in it was not strong enough for gold and jewels. It tried its best, but all it could give the excited people were sacks of cabbages, bags of apples, and bars of chocolate!

"Wicked table!" cried Prince Bong, and drew his sword to slash it. "Horrible table!" cried Queen Puff, and slapped it hard. But that was too much for the frightened table. It jumped up on two legs and began to fight for itself.

Down slid all the dishes, glasses, plates, and knives! The King found a roast chicken in his lap, and Queen Puff was splashed from head to foot with hot gravy. Prince Bong howled when a large ham fell on his toe, and altogether there was a fine to-do.

The table hit out. Slap! That was for the King. Slosh! That was for Prince Bong. Punch! That was for King Piff. Scratch! That was for Queen Puff. Oh, the table soon began to enjoy itself mightily!

But, oh my, the King was calling for his soldiers, and the table could not hope to fight against guns. It suddenly ran down the dining-hall, jumped right over the heads of the astonished soldiers, and disappeared out of the door. How it ran!

"After it, after it!" yelled the King, who did not mean to lose the magic table if he could help it. But the table had vanished into the darkness.

It stumbled on and on, grieving that it could find no place where it would be treated properly. All it wanted was a room with a warm fire, a good polish once each week, and no kicking.

At last it came to a funny-looking shop, lighted inside with one dim lamp. The table peeped in. What a funny collection of things there was there! Old-fashioned furniture, suits of armour, rugs from far countries, lovely vases, old glasses, beaten-brass trays, strange, dusty pictures—oh, I couldn't tell you all there was.

It was a shop kept by an old man who sold strange things. Outside hung a sign on which was written the word "Antiques." The table did not know what that meant. All it knew was that there was a fire at the end of the shop, and that everything looked dusty and old—surely a table could hide here and never be discovered!

It crept in at the door. There was the old man, reading a book as old as himself, and the table hoped he would not look up as it walked softly among the dusty furniture.

"Who's there? Who's there?" said the old man, still

not looking up. " Wait a minute—I must just finish my page, and I'll serve you."

The table squashed itself into a corner by the fire. It put up one of its paws and pulled down an embroidered cloth from  the wall to cover itself. Then it heaved a sigh and stood quite still, enjoying the fire.

When the old man had finished his page he looked up—but there was no one in his shop. How strange!

" I felt sure I heard someone!" he said, rubbing his chin and looking all round, but he could see no one. So he went back to his book, and the table sidled a bit nearer the fire.

From that day to this no one has ever heard of that enchanted table. There it stands, happy and forgotten, in the old furniture shop, warming itself by the fire. If ever you see a round table with little animals carved round its edge, and with four big paws for feet, buy it. It is sure to be the long-lost enchanted table. But *do* be careful how you treat it, won't you?

The Boy Who Boasted

SAMMY was always getting into trouble with the other children because he boasted. I expect you know children who boast, and I'm quite sure you don't like them a bit.

"I've got a bigger kite than anyone in the village," Sammy would say. "And it flies higher than anybody else's! Ho, you should just see it!"

Then, when George brought his new engine to school to show everyone, Sammy boasted again.

"Pooh! That's only a clockwork engine. You should see mine at home. It goes by electricity!"

"Don't boast," said George, feeling suddenly that his engine wasn't so nice as he had thought it was.

But Sammy couldn't seem to stop boasting. "I can run faster than any boy at school!" he boasted to his father. "I can do more sums in half an hour than anyone else. I can write better than anyone in my class."

"Well, it's a pity your school reports aren't better then," said his father. "Stop boasting about what you can do, and *do* something for a change. Then I might believe you."

Now Sammy might have gone on boasting for the rest of his life if something hadn't happened. It's a good thing it did happen, because though it's bad enough to hear a child boasting, it's ten times worse to hear a grown-up doing the same thing. I'll tell you what happened.

One day Sammy was going home from school when he picked up a most peculiar pocket-knife. It was bright yellow, with blue ends, and when Sammy opened the blades, he saw

that they were made of green steel. He stood and stared at the knife, wondering who had lost it. And because he was an honest boy, he looked round to see if he could find the owner. Not far off was someone as small as himself and he was hunting everywhere on the ground.

"Hi, boy!" shouted Sammy. "Have you lost a knife, because I've found one?"

The little fellow looked up—and Sammy couldn't quite make him out. He was as small as a boy and yet he looked more like a grown-up. He was dressed a bit queerly, too, in a green tunic and long stockings, and he wore a pointed hat on his head with a bell at the tip.

"Oh," said the little fellow, "have you found my knife? Thank you! My name is Smink. What's yours?"

"Sammy," said Sammy. "That's a funny-looking knife. I've got one at home. It's better than yours—much sharper. It can cut through wood like butter!"

"Oh, mine's sharper than that," said Smink. "It can cut through a tree-trunk like butter!"

"Fibber!" said Sammy. "You're boasting."

"Well, so are you," said Smink. "But I'm telling the truth and you're not. Look!"

And, to Sammy's enormous surprise, Smink went up to a birch tree, drew his knife right through the trunk, and cut the

tree in half!
Crash! It
fell to the
ground.

Sammy
was
startled.
"Grac-
ious!"
he said.
"That
knife of
yours certainly *is* sharp. But you'll get into trouble if you cut trees down like that."

"I was only showing you," said Smink. He lifted the little tree up again and set it on its trunk. He took a tube of sticky stuff from his pocket and rubbed some on the tree and its trunk. Then it stood upright, looking quite itself again.

"It'll grow all right again," said Smink. "That is Growing-Glue I used. Stronger than any glue you've ever used, I'm sure!"

"Well, at home I've got a tube of glue that will stick all kinds of broken things," said Sammy, beginning to boast again. "It will stick legs on to tables, and backs on to chairs, and . . ."

"Fibber," said Smink. "You haven't any glue strong enough to do that. Now this glue of mine is so strong it would even stick your feet to the ground."

"You're boasting," said Sammy. "I shan't listen to you."

"All right, I'll prove it," said Smink—and quick as light-ning, he tipped Sammy over so that he fell to the ground, and then Smink dabbed a little glue on the sole of each shoe. Sammy jumped to his feet in a rage, meaning to slap Smink—

but, dear me, the little fellow had spoken the truth—Sammy's feet *were* stuck to the ground. He couldn't move a step.

"Oh, oh, my feet won't move!" he shouted in a temper. "Take your glue away."

"Can't," said Smink with a grin. "You'll have to get out of your shoes and leave them behind."

And that's just what poor Sammy had to do! He slipped his feet out of his shoes and ran at Smink in his stockinged feet.

"I'm the strongest boy in my class!" he shouted. "So look out for yourself!"

But Smink was off like the wind. "It won't help you to run away," panted Sammy. "I can run faster than any boy in my school. I'll soon catch you."

"Well, I can run faster than any boy alive!" yelled Smink. And he certainly could. There was no doubt about that at all—he went like the wind. Sammy couldn't possibly catch him. Smink sat down on a grassy bank and let Sammy catch him up that way.

"Now I warn you—don't hit me," said Smink, "because although you may think you can slap harder than anyone in

your village, I can smack harder than any boy anywhere. So be careful."

But Sammy wasn't careful! He gave Smink a slap—and Smink at once jumped up and smacked Sammy so hard that he fell down to the ground and rolled over three times!

" Oooh ! " he said, sitting up. " What hit me then ? "

" I did," said Smink. " Don't say I didn't warn you."

" I'll tell my mother and father about you," said Sammy, beginning to cry. " And you'll be sorry then, because my father and mother are big and strong and they will punish you hard."

" Well, my mother and father are big and strong too," said Smink. " There they are, walking over there. Would you like to see what they do to horrid boys like you ? "

Sammy looked to where Smink pointed—and to his surprise, saw two very tall, rather fierce-looking people walking through the wood. They were so tall that Sammy half-wondered if they could be giants! He decided at once that he didn't want to have anything to do with them.

" Don't call them," he said hurriedly to Smink. " I can see how big and strong they are without them coming any nearer. Where do you live ? "

" In this wood," said Smink. " Where do you ? "

" In the village," said Sammy. " And our house is the biggest one there, and it has the best garden too. And we've got a pond. You should just see it."

" I live in a castle," said Smink. " Our garden is so big that we keep fifty gardeners. And our pond is a lake with a steamer on it."

" Oh, you really are a most dreadful fibber," said Sammy, quite shocked.

" I'll slap you again if you call me a fibber," said Smink. " I don't boast like you. What I say is always true. Come with me and I'll show you."

He dragged Sammy off by the arm—and in a few minutes, to Sammy's enormous astonishment, they came to a great wooden gate let into a high wall. Smink pushed it open—and there, set in the most beautiful grounds, was a real, proper castle with towers and all ! And working in the garden were so many gardeners that Sammy felt there might even be more than fifty !

"Oooh ! There's the lake," he said. "And it really has got a steamer on it. Goodness, aren't you lucky ? Have you got a bicycle or a tricycle to ride ? I've got a wonderful tricycle. I'm sure it's the best in the world. Its bell rings so loudly that everyone gets out of the way at once."

"I'll show you *my* tricycle," said Smink, and he went to a nearby shed. He opened the door and wheeled out a most marvellous tricycle !

"It's made of gold," said Smink, and he got on it. "Out of the way, boy."

He rode straight at Sammy, ringing the bell —and my word, the noise that bell made ! It was like a hundred church bells clanging together at once. Sammy put his hands to his ears and fled out of the way of the swift tricycle.

"Stop ringing the bell !" he cried. "Oh, stop ! It's making me deaf."

Smink stopped. He got off the tricycle and grinned. "Do you want to see anything else?" he asked.

"Well, I must be getting home," said Sammy, feeling that he had seen quite enough for one day. "My puppy-dog will be missing me. I bet you haven't got a pup half as nice as mine. Do you know, mine's got a bark that would frighten any burglar at once, and his teeth are so big and sharp. And run—well, you should just see him! He could run you off your feet any day!"

"Well, I've got a puppy, too," said Smink. "And he's got a marvellous bark. And teeth! Gracious, you should see them! They're so sharp that when he took a dislike to the lawn-mower yesterday, he just chewed it all up! And when he runs you can't see his legs, they go so fast!"

"Oh, don't boast," said Sammy, in disgust. But Smink wasn't going to have Sammy saying that. He went to a big

yard and opened a gate. He whistled—and out of the kennel there came a simply enormous puppy, gambolling round happily. He barked—and it sounded like the crash of a gun! He growled—and it was like the rumbling of a thunderstorm! He showed his enormous teeth, and Sammy shivered. Goodness, yes —this puppy could chew up a lawn-mower and never notice it!

Sammy began to run. He was afraid of that big

puppy. The puppy gambolled after him merrily. Sammy ran faster. The puppy snapped playfully at his ankles. Sammy was simply terrified. He felt certain that the puppy could chew him up just as his own puppy at home had chewed up his father's slipper.

Poor Sammy! He tore home in his stockinged feet, and felt the puppy snapping at his heels the whole way. Not until he was indoors and had slammed the door did he feel safe. He lay on the sofa, panting, his feet without any shoes, and his stockings all in holes.

He told his mother what had happened, and she found it very difficult to believe. " Well, Sammy," she said, " if it's true, you'll have to remember one thing. Never boast again in case you meet another Smink. See what happens when you do! "

So I don't expect he *will* boast again. I guess Smink had a good laugh about it all, don't you?

The Disagreeable Monkey

ONCE upon a time six monkeys lived in a big cage together. They were all brown, they all had funny little faces, and they all had very long tails.

Five of them were good-tempered peaceable creatures, willing to share a banana with one another, or to give each other a monkey-nut. But the sixth monkey—oh, what a disagreeable fellow he was! He was the biggest of the lot, which was a pity, because if he had been *small* and disagreeable nobody would have taken much notice of him—but as he was so big, all the other monkeys were afraid of him.

He was a greedy fellow, Bula, the sixth monkey. When visitors came and poked pieces of orange, banana, or cucumber through the wires, Bula was always there first! Even when his hands and mouth were full of fruit or nut, he still snatched at the other monkeys' tit-bits.

When nobody came to give the monkeys fruit Bula would sit in a corner, sulking. If one of the other monkeys came near him he would snarl, and perhaps chase him. Then round and round the cage they would go, and when at last Bula caught the frightened creature, he would pull handfuls of hair out of him and pinch him cruelly.

So, as you can see, he really was a horrid animal. As for the game of Pulling Tails, nobody was cleverer at it than Bula. You should have seen him creep quietly under the perch on which two or three of the others were sitting, with their long tails dangling down. He would suddenly catch hold of the tails and give them a hearty pull so that all the monkeys screeched and nearly fell off the perch with fright. But Bula never had *his* tail pulled—no, he always curled it neatly round him when he sat on a perch. He didn't let anyone have a chance of pulling it!

The other monkeys didn't know what to do about Bula. They could have been so happy without him. But the keeper came to their help, and what do you think he did? He put a big mirror in the cage one night when the monkeys were asleep! You wouldn't think that would help much, would you? —but you shall hear what happened!

When the monkeys awoke in the morning, one of them saw the mirror. He ran over to it and looked at it. To his enormous astonishment he saw another monkey there—one he had never seen before, for of course he didn't know what he himself looked like!

He ran back to the other monkeys and told them about the new monkey. Bula was still asleep, so they didn't wake him. One by one the other four monkeys crept over to the mirror and peeped in to see the new monkey.

" How cross Bula will be to see there is another monkey! " said the smallest monkey. " He says there are too many of us already! "

" He will give the new monkey a dreadful time," said another. " He will pinch him and pull his tail! "

" Perhaps the new monkey will fight Bula and conquer him! " said the biggest monkey, who had once tried to fight Bula himself and had been beaten.

" Let's tell Bula there is a great big new monkey over there, ready to fight him," said the smallest monkey, excited. "Then he will rush over and start fighting and perhaps the new monkey will beat him. Oh my, what fun that would be! "

" Yes, let's go and tell

him that," said the biggest monkey. So off they went to wake up Bula. He was very cross.

"What do you want?" he chattered angrily. "How dare you wake me up!"

"Oh, Bula, there is a new monkey in our cage," said the biggest monkey. "He is over there. He is bigger than you, and stronger, and he will fight you and make himself our king. Then you will have to sit in a corner all day and say nothing, whilst the stranger takes your tit-bits and pulls your tail."

Well, you should have seen the dreadful face that Bula pulled and heard the awful screech he gave when he heard

this news! He was angrier than he had ever been in his life before!

He rushed off at once to where the monkeys pointed, and came to the looking-glass. He looked in and saw himself—but he didn't know that—he thought there was another monkey there!

"Ugly creature!" he cried. "Disagreeable-looking fellow! What nasty little eyes you have! What a horrid mouth! How dare you come here? Go away at once or I will hit you on the nose!"

The other monkey looked just as angrily at Bula as Bula was looking at him. Bula shook his hairy little fist and the other monkey shook his fist too. That was too much for Bula. With a howl of rage he threw himself on the cheeky monkey—and banged his head dreadfully hard on the glass! He thought the monkey had hit him, and he was so angry that he tried to strike his enemy with both fists at once.

But the other monkey seemed to have a very hard body! Bula's fists were quite sore with hitting against the glass—only to bang his head and bruise his hands. It was most extraordinary.

At last, tired and puzzled, Bula crept away to a corner and hung his head. He couldn't beat that monkey and he was ashamed and sad.

Then the other monkeys went to the looking-glass to praise the winner—and to their great surprise they saw there, not one monkey, but five! They couldn't understand it at all!

"What a marvellous monkey this is!" they cried. "He can turn himself into as many monkeys as he likes. No wonder he was able to beat Bula. Oh, he is a wonderful monkey, the king of all monkeys, and we will tell him so every morning and every night."

They do—and if they go alone, they see only one monkey there—but if they go together they see many, and they bow and scrape very humbly. As for Bula, he has never been near the looking-glass since that strange fight, and he is quite a different monkey now—for, if he looks disagreeable, the others say:

"Ho, Bula! What are you looking like that for? Be pleasant or we will tell our King Monkey to fight you again!"

And the only one who knows the secret is the keeper. Dear me, how he laughs to himself when he sees how much nicer Bula the monkey has become!

The Smickle-Smockle

ANNA HAD a birthday, and her Aunt Jane gave her a lovely box of coloured plasticine. Anna was pleased. She showed the plasticine to the toys.

"It looks like just coloured sticks," she said, "but I can make it into marvellous things. You just watch me!"

She took a stick of red plasticine into her hands and warmed it. Then she began to squeeze it and work it about until she had made it into a round ball. She rolled it across the nursery floor. "There!" she said. "I've made it into a ball! Now watch what I'll make the next stick of plasticine into!"

She took a yellow piece and began to work that about in her hands, too. She squeezed it quite flat, then turned up the sides and smoothed them nicely. "I'm making a cup to drink from," she told the curly-haired doll. "I've just got to make a handle for it then it will be finished. Look— isn't it pretty?"

It really was a sweet little cup. It even held water. The toys watched Anna with the greatest interest. A twinkle came into the golliwog's eyes. He thought it would be fun to do a little work with the plasticine that night—*he* would make something marvellous! Oh yes—Golly always thought he could do wonders!

So that night, when Anna was fast asleep in bed, Golly took the box of plasticine and opened it. He looked at it with his head on one side. What should he make? The toys came round him to see.

"Make a ball," said the pink rabbit, looking at the golly with large glass eyes. "Then I'll play with it."

The pink rabbit was a timid little thing, and Golly was fond of teasing.

"No—I'll make a tiger that will chase you!" he said.

The rabbit squealed. "No, no—I should run away and never come back."

"Then I'll make a red fox with a long bushy tail, and eyes that go like this!" said Golly, making his eyes big, and glaring at the rabbit.

"Oh, don't look like that," said the rabbit, backing away. "Don't! You frighten me. Don't make a fox. I'm afraid of them."

"Well—I'll make an owl, a big hooting owl," said Golly, enjoying himself. "One with great claws that can hold little rabbits, and a voice that goes 'Ooo-ooo-ooo-OOOO!'"

"Sh! Sh!" said the big teddy bear. "You'll wake up Anna, you silly, oooo-ing like that. Be quiet. And don't you dare to make a tiger, or a red fox or an owl. You are not to frighten the pink rabbit."

The pink rabbit had run right away to the other end of the nursery when Golly had hooted like an owl. He had scrambled into the waste-paper basket and hidden himself under some paper. Golly grinned.

" I won't make a tiger, a red fox or a hooting owl," he said to the teddy. " I'll make something else."

So, just behind the toy-cupboard door, he set to work with

the plasticine, and he made a most peculiar animal. It had a small head, enormous ears, a long neck, a perfectly round body with wings, and a long tail like a fish. It had three feet at the front, and what looked like a wheel behind. It really was very queer.

" What is it ? " asked the bear. " I've never seen anything at all like that before."

" It's a smickle-smockle," said the golliwog, with a grin, adding a pair of cat's whiskers to the queer creature.

" Well, it's not very pretty," said the teddy, and went off to play at ball with the other toys. They played until the daylight began to come in at the nursery window.

" Time to get back into the toy cupboard," said the teddy bear. " Come along, everyone. Golly, call the pink rabbit. He's still in the paper basket, and if he doesn't come out, he may be emptied into the dust-bin."

The golly watched all the toys getting into the toy-cupboard, and then he called to the pink rabbit. " Come out ! The sun will soon be up and we must sleep."

The pink rabbit poked his big ears out of the basket. He couldn't see a tiger, a red fox or an owl. So he jumped out and ran over the carpet.

" I've got something to show you," said the golliwog, and

took him behind the cupboard door. There stood the smickle-smockle, looking very fierce because the golly had cleverly pressed two red-headed pins into the head for eyes.

"Oooooh! What is it?" said the poor pink rabbit, trembling.

"It's a smickle-smockle!" said the golly. "Isn't it fierce?"

"What does it eat?" asked the poor pink rabbit, trembling so much that his tail nearly fell off.

"It eats PINK RABBITS!" said the naughty golliwog. The rabbit gave a loud squeal and jumped into the toy-cupboard in such a hurry that he trod on the clockwork mouse and knocked his key out. He scrambled into the back of the cupboard and sat there, trembling. "The smickle-smockle will eat me," he sobbed. "He will, he will!"

" The golliwog is very naughty to tease you like that," said the bear. " Golly, put the plasticine away and come into the cupboard. AT ONCE ! "

The golliwog quickly squashed the smickle-smockle together, and squeezed the plasticine into long sticks again. He put them neatly into the box, ready for Anna to play with once more, and then carried the box into the toy-cupboard.

" I've put the smickle-smockle into the box," he said, with a grin. " I hope he won't get out." ·

" Oh ! Oh ! Don't put the box in here, then, in case he gets out ! " wailed the pink rabbit, and he tried to shut himself into the brick-box.

" He'll get out if he smells a pink rabbit nearby, but not unless," said the naughty golly. That made the pink rabbit go nearly mad, and he rushed round and round the toy-cupboard, squealing loudly. Everyone got very tired of him.

" You've trodden on my face," said the blue cat.

" And you've stepped twice on my tail," said the monkey. " Settle down and sleep, stupid ! Golly, open the box of plasticine and show the pink rabbit that the smickle-smockle really isn't there, for goodness' sake ! "

" No, don't open the box, don't open the box ! " wailed the rabbit. " The smickle-smockle will jump straight out at me if you do ! "

The golly began to open the lid—and the pink rabbit leapt straight out of the cupboard into the coal-scuttle ! And there he had to stay, because by that time it was day, and no toy was allowed to move or speak.

Anna found the pink rabbit in the coal-scuttle, and she had to wash him and peg him up on the line in the garden to dry. He was very unhappy because the pegs hurt his ears. He cried when he got back to the toys that night.

" Oh ! Oh ! Don't put me near the box where the smickle-smockle is ! " he wept, when the teddy bear welcomed him

back. "I can see the box. I shall jump straight into the coal-scuttle again. I shall. I shall!"

"Dear me, this won't do," said the bear, getting quite worried. "Golly, this is all your silly fault. You must think of some way to make the poor pink rabbit feel better. He has had a dreadful shock."

"Yes, Golly. You just put things right," said all the toys; and they looked so stern that the golly quite lost his merry twinkle, and looked scared. It wasn't nice to have every single person against him.

He sat and thought—and then he brightened up.

"I'm going to make some green lettuces, some red carrots, and some yellow onions," he said. "Watch me!"

Everyone watched him. He really was rather clever. He took the green stick of plasticine and made two fine green lettuces. He made three red carrots, and he made five nice yellow onions. They looked lovely.

"There you are, pink rabbit!" said the golly. "That's better than a smickle-smockle, isn't it? *There's* a fine feast for you!"

Well, the little pink rabbit really and truly thought that the golly *had* made him a feast, and before anyone could stop him he ran up to the plasticine vegetables and gobbled up the carrots, the onions and the lettuces! He didn't at all mind that they were plasticine ones. His insides were made of

sawdust, so it wasn't likely that the plasticine would upset him.

" Oh ! " cried the golly in horror. " You've eaten Anna's red, yellow and green plasticine ! There's only the blue and the orange sticks left. Whatever will she say ? "

Well, wasn't that a shock for the toys, especially for Golly ? Most of Anna's plasticine had disappeared into the pink rabbit's tummy !

" You'll have to buy some more," said the bear.

" Where ? " asked Golly, with tears in his eyes. But nobody knew where plasticine could be bought. So they made the golliwog empty out his little money-box and take all his fifteen farthings, and put them into the half-empty box of plasticine for Anna to buy some new bits with. Won't she be surprised when she finds them there.

" Golly won't tease people again in a hurry ! " said the teddy bear. " He can't buy ice-creams for ages now. His money is all gone ! "

It was sad, wasn't it ? Poor Golly didn't smile for at least three nights !

The Golden Enchanter

ONCE upon a time there lived in Shining Palace a
great enchanter. He had thick golden hair, a golden
beard, and always dressed in tunics and cloaks made
of cloth-of-gold. So he was known as the Golden Enchanter.

He was very, very rich. All his plates, dishes, and cups
were made of the purest gold. The very chairs he sat upon
were gold, and the table where he sat for his meals was made
of such heavy gold that it could never be lifted.

In his cellars were sacks upon sacks of gold, but nobody
ever saw them except the Enchanter, for only he had the key
to those dark cellars.

Shining Palace was very beautiful. Its walls were built of
gold, and there were very many windows, all shining and
glittering in the sun that shone every day on the palace. The
Enchanter loved the sun. He used its golden beams in his
magic, and many a bright sunbeam he had imprisoned in his
heavy bars of gold.

The Golden Enchanter was generous and kind-hearted.
He gave much of his gold away, and the people loved him.
But other enchanters were jealous of his riches.

The Green Magician who lived on the next hill envied him
very much, and tried to learn his secrets. The Hobbledy
Wizard was jealous of him too, and wouldn't even speak to
him when he met him. But the Golden Enchanter didn't
mind. He felt sure that his gold was safe, locked up in the
strong cellars.

One day there came to Shining Palace a little, lean man,
whose eyes were a strange green. He asked to see the Enchanter
and he was taken before him.

"Sir," he said, bowing down to the ground, "I have worked for Wily-One, the greatest of magicians, but he has turned me away after twenty years' service. So now I come to you to ask for work. There is not much that I do not know, for Wily-One was clever and taught me most of his secrets."

"Wily-One was wicked," said the Golden Enchanter sternly. "I heard that he had been driven away."

"That may be true," said the green-eyed man. "But listen to all the things I can do, O Enchanter, and I think you will find that I may be very useful to you."

Then, in a long string, the lean man recited all the marvellous spells he could make, and, as he listened, the Enchanter's eyes opened wide.

"I do not know how it was that Wily-One the Magician trusted you so much as to tell you all the secret spells," he said. "Only enchanters are supposed to know them. Well, you must have proved yourself trustworthy to him, so I will engage you to help me. Start to-morrow."

The green-eyed man bowed again, and a strange smile came over his face. The Golden Enchanter did not notice it or he would have wondered about it, and guessed the lean man's secret. For he was no other than Wily-One, the great magician, himself! He had been driven away from his castle, and had had to wander hungry and homeless about the country.

Then he had thought that he would disguise himself and go to the Golden Enchanter to beg for work. Once he was in Shining Palace, surely he could steal the keys of the cellar and help himself to enough gold to make him rich again.

He was delighted when the Enchanter engaged him as his chief helper. Day after day he did magic for him, made strange spells, caught sunbeams for gold, and sang magic words as he stirred the big cauldron on the fire. But he could not get permission to go down into the cellars where the sacks of gold were kept. The Enchanter kept his keys guarded carefully, and slept with them under his pillow. He thought that his new servant was very clever, but he did not like him, nor trust him.

The green-eyed servant lived in a small cottage not far from the palace. One day he found a trap-door in the floor, and lifting it up, spied a small cellar underneath.

" I will keep my potatoes there," he said to himself, and he went down the steps. But when he got there an idea came to him that made him shiver with delight.

" I will use my magic to bore a passage from this cellar to the cellars of Shining Palace," he thought, and he set to work. All day long he worked for the Golden Enchanter, but half the night he worked for himself, bewitching a spade to dig deep into the earth, making a tunnel through the darkness.

At last the tunnel was finished. Wily-One crept through it and came to the small hole leading right into the cellars of Shining Palace. He was delighted. He was just about to crawl through when he heard the sound of footsteps. He crouched down in fear and saw that it was the Golden Enchanter himself, dragging a new sack of gold into place. As Wily-One hid behind the crumbling wall of earth, something tickled his nose. He wanted to sneeze, but he dared not. He held his nose tightly between his finger and thumb, and made the tiniest noise imaginable.

The Golden Enchanter had very quick ears, which could even hear the grass grow in the spring-time. He heard the tiny noise and wondered what it was. He thought it must be the click of a beetle's wings. He dragged the sack into place, and then went to another cellar.

Wily-One thought that he had better not try to steal any gold that night whilst the Enchanter was about. So very quietly he turned and crept back along the dark tunnel to his cottage. He went to bed and dreamed all night long of the large sack of gold he would have on the morrow.

The Enchanter had a great deal of work to do the next day, for there was a very fine and delicate spell he was making. It was mostly made of cobwebs and the whiskers of gooseberries, and all the windows had to be shut in case the wind should blow in and upset the spell.

The green-eyed servant was helping. His eyes shone strangely and his cheeks were red with excitement. He kept thinking of that night, when he would once more have gold of his own and be rich. He would go far away to another country, build himself a fine castle, and be a magician once again.

The Golden Enchanter wondered why his assistant's eyes shone so green, and why his hands trembled when he carefully arranged the cobwebs in the right order.

"What's the matter with you this morning?" he asked. "You don't seem yourself."

"I'm all right," said Wily-One.

"Now for goodness' sake don't sneeze or breathe too hard," said the Enchanter, giving the last touches to the spell. "If you do, all these cobwebs will have to be arranged again."

But one of the gooseberry whiskers must have got up Wily-One's nose, for all of a sudden he wanted to sneeze.

He held his nose tightly between his finger and thumb and stopped the sneeze, making only the very tiniest noise, the same noise that he had made the night before in the cellar.

And the Golden Enchanter remembered the noise.

"So that's what that little noise was last night!" he thought to himself. "It was this green-eyed servant of mine stopping a sneeze. It wasn't a beetle's wings clicking! Oho! I shall have to look into this. Perhaps this clever servant of mine is not what he seems."

The more he thought about it, the more the Enchanter felt sure that his servant was really a magician—and suddenly he guessed Wily-One's secret! Of course—he was Wily-One himself, disguised! Wily-One had those strange green eyes too. However could he, the Golden Enchanter, have been tricked like this?

"I'll hide in the cellars to-night and see what he is up to,"

thought the Enchanter. So that night very early he hid behind his sacks and waited. Just as he had guessed the green-eyed servant crept along the tunnel, climbed into the cellar, and caught up a sack of gold!

"Hi!" shouted the Golden Enchanter. "Put that down,

you robber! I know who you are! You're Wily-One, the wicked magician who was driven away from his castle!"

Wily-One leapt through the hole in a trice and scuttled along the tunnel to his cottage. There he shut down the trapdoor and bolted it so that the Enchanter could not follow him. Then he took a magic broomstick he had once stolen from a witch, and rode away on it, taking the sack of gold with him.

But following him he saw a little bird, whom the Enchanter had ordered to chase Wily-One, for he did not like to leave his palace unguarded. He would call out his guards, bid them surround the palace whilst he was gone, and then follow the wicked magician himself. Meanwhile the little bird tracked Wily-One for him.

Wily-One landed at last in a broad field, so sleepy that he could fly no longer. Dawn was just breaking. He saw the little bird who had followed him wheel round and fly off towards Shining Palace.

"Well, by the time you come back with the Golden Enchanter I shall be gone!" he said. He looked at the sack of gold and decided that he had better bury it instead of taking it with him, for it was heavy. So he bewitched a strong stick and bade it make little holes all over the field. When that was done, he bade each piece of gold hide itself there. In a very short time the thousands of golden pieces were hidden all over the field, and there was none to be seen.

And at that moment Wily-One saw the Enchanter running towards him! In a trice he changed himself into a rabbit and ran away at top speed.

The Enchanter turned himself into a fox and a breathless race began. Just as the rabbit was almost caught Wily-One changed himself into a lark. Up and up into the sky he rose, hoping to get away from the Enchanter.

But the Enchanter turned himself into an eagle and soared

swiftly after the lark. Down the sky they went, the lark trying its hardest to escape. But with a downward rush the eagle was upon it, and both dropped to the earth. As they touched the ground Wily-One turned himself into a tiny mouse, hoping to hide among the bracken. But the Enchanter turned himself into a big black cat and began to hunt the mouse here and there. Smack! It clapped its great paw on to the mouse's back, and knowing himself so nearly caught Wily-One changed swiftly into a snake and tried to bite the cat.

In a trice the Enchanter changed back into his own shape and struck the snake with a stick. It glided away and came to a deep pond. The Enchanter followed and lifted his stick again. Hey presto! Wily-One changed into a big fish and slipped silently into the water.

The Enchanter became an otter and slid into the water after him. Round and round the pond they swam, the fish twisting and turning in fear lest the otter should bite him in the neck.

Just as the otter pounced, the fish leapt into the air and changed into a brown bear. He clambered out of the water and ran to the mountains. The otter climbed out after him and changed into a bear too. He raced after his enemy, growling fiercely.

Wily-One saw a cave in a hillside and ran inside. In a trice the Golden Enchanter changed from a bear back to his own shape and laughed loudly. He took a great stone and rolled it in front of the cave, pinning it there by the most powerful magic he knew.

"Well, there you are, and there you may stay!" said he. "I would never let a wicked magician like you free, for you do so much harm. No, here you will stay for hundreds of years and perhaps you will find time to repent."

With that he left him and went back to Shining Palace. He did not bother to look for the stolen gold, for he had so much that he hardly missed it.

But one day he happened to pass the field where Wily-One had hidden the gold—and he stared in wonder and delight! Each little gold piece had taken root and grown! The plants had flowered in thousands all over the field and were waving their bright golden heads in the sunshine.

"I've never seen anything so beautiful in my life!" said the Enchanter. "I hope the seeds will spread, so that the flowers may be seen by everybody!"

They did spread—they spread all over the world, and now each summer-time you may see fields full of the bright golden flowers that once grew from the stolen gold. Do you know what we call them? Yes, buttercups, of course!

As for Wily-One, he is still in the cave, and long may he remain there!

The Wizard's Umbrella

RIBBY the Gnome lived in a small cottage at the end of Tiptoe Village. Nobody liked him because he was always borrowing things and never bringing them back ! It was most annoying of him.

The things he borrowed most were umbrellas. I really couldn't tell you how many umbrellas Ribby had borrowed in his life—hundreds, I should think ! He had borrowed Dame Twinkle's nice red one, he had taken Mr. Biscuit the Baker's old green one, he had had Pixie Dimple's little grey and pink sunshade, and many, many more.

If people came to ask for them back, he would hunt all about and then say he was very sorry but he must have lent their umbrellas to someone else—he certainly hadn't got them in his cottage now. And no one would ever know what had happened to their nice umbrellas !

Of course, Ribby the Gnome knew quite well where they were! They were all tied up tightly together hidden in his loft. And once a month, Ribby would set out on a dark night, when nobody was about, and take with him all the borrowed umbrellas. He would go to the town of Here-we-are, a good many miles away, and then the next day he would go through the streets there, crying : " Umbrellas for sale ! Fine umbrellas ! "

He would sell the whole bundle, and make quite a lot of money. Then the wicked gnome would buy himself some fine new clothes, and perhaps a new chair or some new curtains for his cottage and go home again.

Now one day it happened that Dame Twinkle went over

to the town of Here-we-are, and paid a call on her cousin, Mother Tantrums. And there standing in the umbrella-stand in Mother Tantrum's hall, Dame Twinkle saw her very own nice red umbrella, that she had lent to Ribby the Gnome the month before!

She stared at it in great surprise. However did it come to be in her cousin's umbrella-stand? Surely she hadn't lent it to Mother Tantrums? No, no—she was certain, quite certain, she had lent it to Ribby the Gnome.

"What are you staring at?" asked Mother Tantrums in surprise.

"Well," said Dame Twinkle, pointing to the red umbrella, "it's a funny thing, Cousin Tantrums, but, you know, that's my red umbrella you've got in your umbrella-stand."

"Nonsense!" said Mother Tantrums. "Why, that's an umbrella I bought for a shilling from a little gnome who often comes round selling things."

"A *shilling*!" cried Dame Twinkle in horror. "My goodness, gracious me, I paid sixteen shillings and ninepence for it! A shilling, indeed! What next!"

"What are you talking about?" asked Mother Tantrums, quite cross. "It's *my* umbrella, not yours—and a very good bargain it was, too!"

"I should think so!" said Dame Twinkle, looking lovingly

at the red umbrella, which she had been very fond of indeed. "Tell me, Cousin, what sort of a gnome was this that sold you your umbrella?"

"Oh, he was short and rather fat," said Mother Tantrums.

"Lots of gnomes are short and fat," said Dame Twinkle. "Can't you remember anything else about him?"

"Well, he wore a bright yellow scarf round his neck," said Mother Tantrums, "and his eyes were a very light green."

"That's Ribby the Gnome!" cried Dame Twinkle, quite certain. "He always wears a yellow scarf, and his eyes are a very funny green. Oh, the wicked scamp! I suppose he borrows our umbrellas in order to sell them when he can! Oh, the horrid little thief! I shall tell the wizard who lives in our village and ask him to punish Ribby. Yes, I will! He deserves a very nasty punishment indeed!"

So when she went back to Tiptoe Village, Dame Twinkle went to call on the Wizard Deep-one. He was a great friend of hers, and when he heard about Ribby's wickedness he shook his head in horror.

"He must certainly be punished," said the wizard, nodding his head. "Leave it to me, Dame Twinkle. I will see to it."

Deep-one thought for a long time, and then he smiled. Ha, he would lay a little trap for Ribby that would teach him never to borrow umbrellas again. He took a spell and with it he made a very fine umbrella indeed. It was deep blue, and for a handle it had a dog's head. It was really a marvellous umbrella.

The wizard put it into his umbrella-stand and then left his front door open wide every day so that anyone passing by could see the dog's-head umbrella quite well. He was sure that Ribby the Gnome would spy it the very first time he came walking by.

When Ribby did see the umbrella he stopped to have a good look at it. My, what a lovely umbrella! He hadn't noticed it before, so it must be a new one. See the dog's head

on it, it looked almost real! Oh, if Ribby could only get *that* umbrella, he could sell it for a good many shillings in the town of Here-we-are. He was sure that the enchanter who lived there would be very pleased to buy it.

" Somehow or other I must get that umbrella," thought Ribby. " The very next time it rains I will hurry by the wizard's house, and pop in and ask him to lend it to me! I don't expect he will, but I'll ask, anyway!"

So on the Thursday following, when a rainstorm came, Ribby hurried out of his cottage without an umbrella and ran to Deep-one's house. The front door was wide open as usual and Ribby could quite well see the dog-headed umbrella in the hall-stand. He ran up the path, and knocked at the open door.

" Who's there? " came the wizard's voice.

" It's me, Ribby the Gnome! " said the gnome. " Please, Wizard Deep-one, could you lend me an umbrella? It's pouring with rain and I am getting so wet. I am sure I shall get a dreadful cold if someone doesn't lend me an umbrella."

" Dear, dear, dear! " said the wizard, coming out of his parlour, and looking at the wet gnome. " You certainly are *very* wet! Yes, I will lend you an umbrella—but mind, Ribby, let me warn you to bring it back to-morrow in case something unpleasant happens to you."

"Oh, of course, of course," said Ribby. "I always return things I borrow, Wizard. You shall have it back to-morrow as sure as eggs are eggs."

"Well, take that one from the hall-stand, Ribby," said the wizard, pointing to the dog's-head umbrella. Ribby took it in delight. He had got what he wanted. How easy it had been after all! He, ho, he wouldn't bring it back to-morrow, not he! He would take it to the town of Here-we-are as soon as ever he could and sell it to the enchanter there. What luck!

He opened it, said thank you to the smiling wizard, and rushed down the path with the blue umbrella. He was half afraid the wizard would call him back—but no, Deep-one let him go without a word—but he chuckled very deeply as he saw the gnome vanishing round the corner. How easily Ribby had fallen into the trap!

Of course Ribby didn't take the umbrella back next day. No, he put it up in his loft and didn't go near the wizard's house at all. If he saw the wizard in the street he would pop into a shop until he had gone by. He wasn't going to let him have his umbrella back for a moment!

Now after three weeks had gone by, and Ribby had heard

nothing from the wizard about his umbrella, he decided it would be safe to go to Here-we-are and sell it.

"I expect the wizard has forgotten all about it by now," thought Ribby. "He is very forgetful."

So that night Ribby packed up three other umbrellas, and tied the wizard's dog-headed one to them very carefully. Then he put the bundle over his shoulder and set out in the darkness. Before morning came he was in the town of Here-we-are, and the folk there heard him crying out his wares in a loud voice.

"Umbrellas for sale! Fine umbrellas for sale! Come and buy!"

Ribby easily sold the other three umbrellas he had with him and then he made his way to the enchanter's house. The dog-headed umbrella was now the only one left.

The enchanter came to the door and looked at the umbrella that Ribby showed him. But as soon as his eye fell on it he drew back in horror.

"Buy that umbrella!" he cried. "Not I! Why, it's alive!"

"Alive!" said Ribby, laughing scornfully. "No, sir, it is as dead as a door-nail!"

"I tell you, that umbrella is *alive*!" said the enchanter and he slammed the door in the astonished gnome's face.

Ribby looked at the dog-headed umbrella, feeling very much puzzled—and as he looked, a very queer feeling came over him. The dog's head really did look alive. It wagged one ear as Ribby looked at it, and then it showed its teeth at the gnome and growled fiercely!

My goodness! Ribby was frightened almost out of his life! He dropped the umbrella on to the ground and fled away as fast as his fat little legs would carry him!

As soon as the umbrella touched the ground a very peculiar thing happened to it. It grew four legs, and the head became bigger. The body was made of the long umbrella part, and the tail was the end bit. It could even wag!

"Oh, oh, an umbrella-dog!" cried all the people of Here-we-are town and they fled away in fright. But the strange dog took no notice of anyone but Ribby the Gnome. He galloped after him, barking loudly.

He did look queer. His umbrella-body flapped as he went along on his stout little doggy legs, and his tongue hung out of his mouth. It was most astonishing. People looked out of their windows at it, and everyone closed their front doors with a bang in case the strange umbrella-dog should come running into their houses.

Ribby was dreadfully frightened. He ran on and on, and every now and then he looked round.

"Oh, my goodness, that umbrella-dog's still after me!" he panted. "What shall I do? Oh, why, why, why did I borrow the wizard's umbrella? Why didn't I take it back? I might have known there would be something queer about it!"

The umbrella-dog raced on, and came so near to Ribby that it was able to snap at his twinkling legs. Snap! The dog's sharp teeth took a piece out of Ribby's green trousers!

"Ow! Ooh! Ow!" shrieked Ribby in horror, and he shot on twice as fast, panting like a railway train going up a hill! Everybody watched from their windows and some of them laughed because it was really a very peculiar sight.

Ribby looked out for someone to open a door so that he could run in. But every single door was shut. He must just run on and on. But how much longer could he run? He was getting terribly out of breath.

The umbrella-dog was enjoying himself very much. Ho, this was better fun than being a dull old umbrella! This was seeing life! If only he could catch that nasty little running thing in front, what fun he would have!

The umbrella-dog ran a bit faster and caught up Ribby once more. This time he jumped up and bit a piece out of the gnome's lovely yellow scarf. Then he jumped again and nipped a tiny piece out of Ribby's leg.

" OW ! " yelled Ribby, jumping high into the air. " OW ! You horrid cruel dog! Leave me alone! How dare you, I say? Wait till I get home and find a whip! "

The dog sat down to chew the piece he had bitten out of Ribby's yellow scarf, and the gnome ran on, hoping that the dog would forget about him.

" Oh, if only I could get home! " cried the panting gnome. " Once I'm in my house I'm safe! "

He ran on and on, through the wood and over the common that lay between the town of Here-we-are and the village of Tiptoe. The dog did not seem to be following him. Ribby kept looking round but there was no umbrella-dog there. If only he could get home in time!

Just as he got to Tiptoe Village he heard a pattering of feet behind him. He looked round and saw the umbrella-dog just behind him. Oh, what a shock for poor Ribby!

" Look, look! " cried everyone in surprise. " There's a mad umbrella-dog after Ribby. Run, Ribby, run! "

Poor Ribby had to run all through the village of Tiptoe to get to his cottage. The dog ran at his heels snapping every now and again, making the gnome leap high into the air with pain and fright.

"I'll never, never, never borrow an umbrella again, or anything else!" vowed the gnome, as the dog nipped his heel with his sharp teeth. "Oh, why didn't I take the wizard's umbrella back?"

At last he was home. He rushed up the path, pushed the door open and slammed it. But, alas, the umbrella-dog had slipped in with him, and there it was in front of Ribby, sitting up and begging.

"OH, you horror!" shouted Ribby, trying to open the door and get out again. But the dog wouldn't let him. Every time Ribby put his hand on the handle of the door it jumped up and nipped him. So at last he stopped trying to open it and looked in despair at the strange dog, who was now sitting up and begging.

"Do you want something to eat?" said the gnome.

"Goodness, I shouldn't have thought an umbrella-dog could be hungry. Wait a bit. I've a nice joint of meat here, you shall have that, if only you will stop snapping at me!"

The dog ran by Ribby as he went hurriedly to his larder and opened the door. He took a joint of meat from a dish and gave it to the dog, which crunched it up hungrily.

Then began a very sorrowful time for Ribby! The dog wouldn't leave him for a moment and the gnome had never in his life known such a hungry creature. Although its body was simply an umbrella, it ate and ate and ate. Ribby spent all his money on food for it, and in the days that came, often

went hungry himself. The dog wouldn't leave his side, and when the gnome went out shopping the strange creature always went with him, much to the surprise and amusement of all the people in the village.

"Look!" they would cry. "Look! There goes Ribby the gnome and his queer umbrella-dog! Where did he get it from? Why does he keep such a strange, hungry creature?"

If Ribby tried to creep off at night, or run away from the dog, it would at once start snapping and snarling at his heels, and after it had nibbled a bit out of his leg once or twice and bitten a large hole in his best coat, Ribby gave up trying to go away.

"But what shall I do?" wondered the little gnome, each night, as he looked at his empty larder. "This dog is eating everything I have. I shall soon have no money left to buy anything."

Ribby had had such a shock when the stolen umbrella had turned into the queer umbrella-dog, that he had never once thought of borrowing anything else. He felt much too much afraid that what he borrowed would turn into something like the dog, and he really couldn't bear that!

"I suppose I'd better get some work to do," he said to himself at last. "But who will give me a job? Nobody likes me because I have always borrowed things and never taken them back. Oh dear, how foolish and stupid I have been."

Then at last he thought he had better go to the Wizard Deep-one and confess to him all that had happened. Perhaps Deep-one would take away the horrid umbrella-dog and then Ribby would feel happier. So off he went to the wizard's house.

The wizard opened the door himself and when he saw Ribby with the dog he began to laugh. How he laughed! He held his sides and roared till the tears ran down his cheeks.

"What's the matter?" asked Ribby, in surprise. "What is the joke?"

"*You* are!" cried the wizard, laughing more than ever. "Ho, ho, Ribby, little did you think that I had made that dog-headed umbrella especially for you to borrow and that I knew exactly what was going to happen! Well, you can't say that I didn't warn you. My only surprise is that you haven't come to me before for help. You can't have liked having such a strange umbrella-dog living with you, eating all your food, and snapping at your heels every moment! But it's a good punishment for you—you won't borrow things and not bring them back again, I'm sure!"

"I never, never will," said Ribby, going very red. "I am very sorry for all the wrong things I have done. Perhaps I had better keep this umbrella-dog to remind me to be honest, Wizard."

"No, I'll have it," said Deep-one. "It will do to guard my house for me. I think any burglar would run for miles if he suddenly saw the umbrella-dog coming for him. And what are *you* going to do, Ribby? Have you any work?"

"No," said Ribby, sorrowfully. "Nobody likes me and I'm sure no one will give me any work to do in case I borrow something and don't return it, just as I used to do."

"Well, well, well," said the wizard, and his wrinkled eyes looked kindly at the sad little gnome. "You have learned your lesson, Ribby, I can see. Come and be my gardener and grow my vegetables. I shall work you hard, but I shall pay you well, and I think you will be happy."

So Ribby is now Deep-one's gardener, and he works hard from morning to night. But he is happy because everyone likes him now—and as for the umbrella-dog, he is as fond of Ribby as anyone else is and keeps at his heels all the time. And the funny thing is that Ribby likes him there!